Vie for the Throne

Throne

A FAIRYTALE OF COURAGE

Ancient race, love, and an empty throne.
What's next for a solitary being?

Abbian Yadon

PAGE PUBLISHING, INC.
New York, NY

First originally published by Page Publishing, Inc. 2018

ISBN 978-1-64350-987-7 (Paperback)
ISBN 978-1-64350-988-4 (Digital)

Printed in the United States of America

The boy who helped give me the greatest joy I've ever known, you're a dick, but I love you for it to a very fine point

The man who loved me and was my best friend, I'm so sorry

The woman who's shown me what it is to be yourself and still be an adult, that doesn't go there

My best friend, why are we always so busy?

D, I still don't like strawberry jam

To you both, it's not smut!

My mother, for putting up with me

My dad for loving me with a firm quietness

My other mom, for being my second mom

My son, for being my joy and cuddling me all those midnights when I was up writing

My all writing and English teachers

Mrs. Sanders and Mr. Valentine, who pushed me to keep writing and complained when my assignments were five pages longer than necessary

My best friend Sienna, again, who after all this time still loves me and encourages me

The Lord, who halfway through this book saved me

To me ... you did it

At the Start

Wild animals are not meant to be kept in cages.

One moment, she would be the happiest person in the world. The next, she was about to burst into tears at a second's notice. She was angry, hurt, and rebellious. Then she was happy, carefree, and energetic.

She didn't know how to deal with them.

She was a wild animal that couldn't be contained anymore. It had to be let out.

She ran out of the room.

The teacher screamed after her, "Dihni!"

Instead of heeding the teacher's call, Dihni jumped onto the bridge that ran from one corridor to the next. Lifting her arms, she stood, feet and feet shoulder width apart.

Dihni knew not how long she stood there. All she knew was the wind whipping her hair about, rushing across her body and the feeling of being free.

The sun crept up her legs and hastened to cover her entirely. When it hit her face, she opened her eyes and gasped at the sight before her.

Sunrise was beautiful here. Nowhere in the world could compare to the raw beauty that home in England had always provided her.

A sound like that of a faint whisper that you hear in a memory pervaded her senses.

She was falling back to earth.

No, she thought, *please, just a little longer.*

But someone was softly saying her name.

"Dihni, Dihni, come back. Come back." Over and over, they pleaded with her.

Like slowly sinking wings, her arms started to fall back to her sides, compelled by gravity.

She looked down. A crowd of students had gathered and were looking up at her.

"Dihni."

She turned and looked to her left.

A boy was standing there. He was the one saying her name.

His black hair was a messy mop over variscite eyes laced with silver. His skin was pale and shone in the light as if it was made from opal.

The way Dihni's did.

She hadn't met anyone with skin as opalescent as hers, yet here he was.

Dihni was captured and couldn't look away.

"That's it. Come on down."

He took her hand and gently led her down to stand next to him.

"There you go."

Never had a boy looked like he did to her. He was handsome, yes, but there was something else. She had never seen this in another person.

But what was it?

His eyes never left hers.

"There we are, now how about we go to the gardens and sit for a while?"

She nodded slowly.

He looked up from her then to all the people she could feel around them. Their astonished gazes bore into her although she could not see them.

"Go back to class."

The demanding tone in his voice made Dihni wonder who he thought he was.

He looked down at her; she was a head shorter than him, the top of her head just meeting his chin.

Wrapping his arm around her shoulders, he guided her away.

Her eyes were transfixed upon him.

He glanced down at her. "How about we go somewhere no one goes so we can get you away from people? I'm going to need you to close your eyes though. This place is secret. Can you do that? Close your eyes."

Dihni slowly closed her eyes and faced forward.

He kept them at a steady pace but didn't rush. The sound of people shuffling around them was almost deafening.

Everywhere murmuring and little intakes of breath could be heard. It was like listening to the echoes of ghosts.

A cold shiver ran down Dihni's whole body, right down to her toes.

"Hey, it's okay. We're almost there. Don't worry, I got you."

Then the voices faded, and then they were gone, replaced by the sound of the breeze blowing through the outer corridor.

The smell of flowers, trees, and freshly cut grass was intoxicating. She heard water flowing and birds chirping, leaves rustling against one another. Then she felt the sun warming her.

It was impossible to stop a sigh of satisfaction from escaping her lips.

The boy laughed. It was a pleasant laugh, deep and filled with amusement and some other emotion that was not identifiable. Could it have been incredulity?

"You're happy now? Wait until you open your eyes." Dihni started to do just that, and he cried out, "Wait, not yet!" putting his hand over her eyes.

Her eyelids relaxed again.

They then made a series of turns and twists, and their pace quickly began to be hastened. There were so many turns and twists, coupled with their speed, that she started to get dizzy. So dizzy, in fact, that on one of the turns, she almost fell. He laughed and caught her saying that he would slow down only a little.

There was only one place on campus that had that many turns in it.

They were in the maze.

It was said that in the middle was a beautiful garden, but no one could find it because the maze was so big and hard to navigate for the sameness of the bush walls. Not even she had found her way into the middle. She had tried racing over the walls like a cat once, but she ended up scaring a real cat and fell.

She smiled.

They slowed to a halting stop.

What happened? Are we there already?

Then she felt fingers brush her cheek. She flinched.

"I'm sorry. I just … never mind. Almost there."

They made a few odd curving steps. Then she felt the ground below her feet smooth out and slowly rise.

He stopped her. "Okay. Open your eyes."

Dihni did so and gasped.

They were in circular garden.

The Garden's Enchantments

Flowers were planted everywhere, so many that you couldn't even identify all of them. The air was filled with the scent of them. A light breeze made the little flowers bob and dance, making them look animated.

Stone paths wound through the flowers, and swinging benches were set up in a few areas. Below them was a massive pond, big enough to be a public pool. The water was clear, the stones on the bottom visible, at least, until five feet away from the edge; from then on, the water was dark. Fish were swimming among the water lilies and other aquatic plants.

Under their feet was an elaborate dark wood bridge. Cherry blossom trees dotted the garden, along with apple trees and white blossoms. The trees were so old they might as well have been oak trees for their size.

How can something so beautiful exist in a place like this unattended?

Turning to the boy, she just looked at him. He had a small smile on his face, and his eyes were bright. "Do you like it?"

Dihni could only look at him, astounded.

He fidgeted. "Now would be a good time to say something."

Dihni had not said a word out loud for a very long time, and she honestly didn't remember how to start. It was not something she really wanted to do anyways.

His smile slowly drooped. "Can't you talk?"

She nodded.

"Then why don't you?"

All around the garden her eyes searched, trying to figure out how to explain.

Then it came to her.

What a better way to explain something than with something else, now to find an example.

On the ground by the bridge was a patch of daisies; one of the daisies was apart from a smaller group of the little white blossoms.

Grabbing his hand, she pulled him off the bridge and over to the little group of flowers.

Pulling him down with her, Dihni pointed to the lone daisy then to her.

Can't you see that I am apart from everyone else? That I am alone?

He frowned. "Living in a world without others is lonely and silent. I get it."

A small smile pervaded her lips.

Then Dihni stood, walking to an apple tree she had noticed in her search for a metaphor of herself. Way up in the tree was a lone apple, and it was perfect. She looked at the rest of the tree then up at the apple again. It was, in fact, the only apple in the tree.

"You want that one? I can get it for you."

He started to climb the tree, but Dihni stopped him with a touch on the shoulder.

Jumping, she grabbed a branch pulling her legs up and around it then swung around and grabbed another branch sitting upright.

She proceeded to shimmy up the tree. It was a big apple tree and had many branches, so instead of going straight up, Dihni decided to take her time and make a twisting route around the tree.

Finally, she reached the top and grabbed the apple, standing on a branch as though she was on a balance beam.

She smiled down at the boy.

He was grinning. "Never mind!"

Tossing the apple down to him, he caught hold of it with one hand smoothly.

Dihni was quietly impressed.

When Dihni looked back up, she was astonished to see another perfect apple not too far away. Reaching for it hesitantly, Dihni grabbed it before she climbed down.

When she got to the last branch, she hung upside down, her legs wrapped around the thick branch.

He had a look of amusement upon his face as he held up the apple. "Why, thank you, monkey."

A warning look is all he got in response.

He laughed. "Okay, fine, Dihni."

She swung on the branch, lightly touched the ground and stood, then motioned from him to her, then from her to him, shrugging her shoulders.

"I know your name, but you don't know mine, right? Thought so, my name is Adler. Adler Gifni." He made a motion much like a stage bow.

She smiled. *Eagle.* Dihni inclined her head, closing her eyes, and then lifted her head, opening her eyes.

Adler had a strange half smile on his face.

She gave him an incredulous look.

He shook his head. "You're so different. It's refreshing."

Dihni took it as a compliment.

The rest of the day was spent as a tour of the garden. Adler showed Dihni every type of plant in it. She dares not tell him that she already knew all that because he was so happy to share with her that it was charming and plain old cute.

Dihni personally spent at least an hour in the sunshine simply lying among the flowers.

They ate their fill of apples and some of the other edible plants. It was a perfect way to spend one's time, so peaceful, bliss.

Dihni was currently seated in one of the swinging benches munching on yet another apple.

Then Adler took her hand, pulling her up. "It's time to go."

She ripped her hand out of his and stepped back.

He looked at her with a sad smile. "I don't want to leave either, but we have to go back to the real world. We've already missed half the day of school."

School was not her main worry.

Looking up, Dihni saw that the sun had moved to the other side of the sky.

A single tear slid down her face. No. *How could it be so late?*

She shook her head, still looking at the sky.

Then she looked at Adler.

As another tear rolled down her cheek, he rushed up to her, wiping the tears from her face with his thumbs, while the rest of his fingers cupped her face and threaded through her hair.

He looked just as disappointed as she felt.

"Please don't cry. We can come back tomorrow."

Dihni raised her hand to his face. She couldn't believe what she was about to do. Why was she about to do this?

Dihni spoke the first words she had spoken in months. "This has been the best day I've had in a long time. I don't want it to end. Words cannot explain the depth of my gratitude, nor the depth of my sorrow that it must end."

The voice that issued from her lips was deep, wise, and filled with emotions. Most people shrank away from her when they heard it, which was why she rarely spoke.

Adler looked deep into her eyes. "Don't ever go silent on me again. I don't think I can go another day without hearing you speak."

Could she really do this? Could she give someone this privilege when she had only just met them? Why did she want to?

When Dihni said nothing in response, he quickly said, "Promise me, Dihni." His grip on her face tightened for a moment.

No more hiding.

Dihni wrapped her arms around him, cupping the back of his head with her hand and pulling him close. He buried his face against her neck.

"I will speak for you. But I cannot promise the absence of silence. Sometimes silence is needed in life. Otherwise, the noise of the world would drown us."

After Adler had held her tightly for a while, he then reluctantly let her go and held her hand on the way out.

As Adler navigated the maze in front of her, she began to wonder how he had gotten her to speak. How he had pulled her out of her barriers?

No one should have been able to do this. She should not have let her guard down. Just because a boy paid attention to you for a day and treated you like you were the greatest person in the world did not mean you had to let your guard down for them; if anything, it meant that you needed to make them stronger.

Dihni stopped, suddenly angry and frightened.

Adler turned and looked frightened. "You okay?"

"No. What do you want from me? How is it that you have managed to make me speak to you? How do you know my name? What do you want from me? I have nothing to give."

Adler looked hurt and stricken; his voice was quiet and sad when he spoke. "Do you really believe that I am being kind to you for my own gain?"

When Dihni said nothing, he continued.

"I saw you slowly slipping farther and farther from the world. I saw you the first day you came here, and I couldn't look away. I started to follow you. I kept people who wanted to hurt you and say mean things about you away. I have kept watch over you every day."

Dihni turned away from him and started to cry. The pain that was written all over him was too much.

"I know your name because I asked students who are in class with you what your name was, and when they didn't know, I asked one of your teachers. I know that you never let your head down. I know that you sit up straight. When the teacher calls on you, you say nothing but write it down. I know that during lunch, you go to the abandoned half of the castle and dance to the music on your phone, which I never see you use other than for music, which means you have no one to talk to. I know that your hair is naturally curly and that there is one strand of hair in front that always falls in front of your face. I know the way it swishes just below your lower back when you walk. I want nothing from you other than your attention.

"I know that someone had hurt you to make you block yourself from the world, and I can promise you that I would never ever do that to you. I know the leather jacket and black clothes and devilish look throw me off, but so does your look. You wear clothes made out of animal hides when you don't have to dress like everyone else, I've seen you. And when you do have to dress like everyone else, you wear clothes that you can move in. You don't dress for style. Who wears leggings and a raincoat that is two sizes too big? No one but you. Your converses are faded and old. Your backpack is brand-new, along with your clothes. I know *about* you, but I don't know *you*.

"I want to know you, Dihni. When I saw you jump on that bridge, I knew you wanted out of all the hurt that this world has caused you, and I couldn't let that happen. Or else, I would have to jump with you. You need someone who shows you that they care about you. Honestly and truly, and I plan to be that person. Don't push me away. I won't come to you, you can come to me whenever you want me around. I won't force you into anything, just please don't push me away."

Dihni had her hand over her mouth. By the time he was done, Dihni was sobbing silently and was shaking all over.

She couldn't stand anymore.

Her knees gave out, and she thumped down, sitting with her legs under her, one hand in front to hold her up.

Adler placed a hand on her back and knelt in front of her. He took her arm with his other hand and pulled her to him.

Time had no right to be in this place, and it left them alone. Dihni had no idea how long he held her, smoothing her hair and holding her close. It felt like forever, and by the time her sobs were reduced to sniffles and hiccupping, she was freezing and it was dark.

Her head felt slightly damp.

She looked up at Adler and discovered that his face was tear streaked. He wiped her tears away with his thumbs again, brushing her hair out of her face.

"I can't bear to see you hurt like this. It hurts me to see it."

Dihni didn't know what to say. Nothing came to mind. So instead of words, she wiped his tears away, held each side of his face, and kissed his forehead.

Adler kept her head above his as he held her, putting his head down on her shoulder with a light thump.

Then he sighed. "We should to go to our rooms. Though I don't want to leave you."

Dihni took a deep breath. "There are worse things than being separated for short times. I will be fine." The fact she was reassuring him felt strange and comforting at the same time. "If it helps, I keep a dagger under my pillow. No one can harm me, and I gave up on harming myself long ago." At that, Adler stiffened. "When the sun goes down, you can always count on it rising on the other side of the world."

Adler looked up at her and deep into her eyes and face, searching for something. Finally, he nodded and then stood up lifting her off the ground, and then gently setting her back down.

It seemed as though they had to stay connected because they could not let go of the others hand. They walked as such all the way to the students' corridors. There was almost no one out, and the few people they did see did not take any notice of them for being too wrapped up in other things, literally.

Just the Beginning

The rest of the school year was spent as such. They would go to the garden every day, skipping most of their classes. Even when it snowed, they went to the garden, bringing hot drinks and thick wool blankets.

It struck Dihni that it was a very rare taste to like wool blankets. They were almost always scratchy and were heavy. Every once in a while, you would get a wool blanket that actually smelled like whatever animal had been sheered to make it.

Almost all of Dihni's blankets were made of wool. She only had two very fluffy and fuzzy blankets that were made that century.

In the heart of summer, they went to the garden, as usual. The sun beat down its unrelenting rays. It was as if the very air were on fire.

Mornan Castle was like an oven. The students who stayed during the summer spent most of their time outside. The forest half of the property students used to camp in because the trees' shade provided the only relief from the heat.

If only there was a way we could cool off, Dihni thought wistfully.

She smiled, then bent down, and took her shoes and socks off.

"Uh, Dihni? What are you doing?"

While still bent down, she reached forward quickly and untied his shoes. He danced away, only untying them more.

"Ah! No. These shoes stay on!"

Dihni laughed softly, walking past him. The silky grass was cool and moist. Walking to the pond, she stepped into the cool water. Her steps light and sure-footed.

"Your pants are going to get wet!"

She discarded the comment with a dismissive wave of her hand. The water swirled around her ankles. It was so cool and felt like silk.

Then something started tickling her toes. Looking down, she couldn't help but laugh at the sight before her eyes.

"What's so funny?"

Dihni jumped, he was standing right behind her.

He looked down at her toes. What he saw was a multitude of little fish swimming around her feet and ankles, kissing her, rubbing up against her.

Adler laughed. "It seems as though you are a favorite. They won't come near me."

Indeed, there were no fish around him.

Looking out across the water, she wondered what would happen if they dove into the depths of the pool. What kind of creatures might be there? She thought she saw something move in the depths.

Adler grabbed her forearm. "I wouldn't. I don't know how deep that water is or what's in there."

She looked over at him. Adler's face was twisted up. It took a moment for Dihni to identify it.

He's afraid, Dihni thought with wonder.

Instead of jumping into the water like she wanted to, she decided not to distress Adler any more than he already was and stayed right where she stood.

Then she bent down, as if to try to touch the little fish, but instead scooped at the water and splashed at Adler.

"Aah! Hey, no fair!"

"Who said there was such a thing as fair?" Dihni laughed, beaming.

Then Adler bent down and scooped water up at her. Dihni shrieked and threw up her hands as if she could stop the water from splashing her.

They splashed each other until they were both absolutely soaked, at which point they kept on going even though the wet clothes were a little uncomfortable.

Adler threw up his hands as she continuously splashed him using two hands. "Okay, okay! You win!"

Dihni threw up her hands and did a little victory dance. Little did she know that Adler had snuck up on her. In her surprise, she jumped back a little.

He lifted his hand, offering it to her. She hesitantly took it, half expecting him to pull a trick. Instead, he led her out of the water.

"I think a dry set of clothes would be appropriate. Wouldn't want to get a cold."

Dihni thought for a moment. It was practically nighttime now. That meant they had played in the water for hours. The student corridors were chilled in the afternoon, whereas her room was very warm. The feeling of her soft, warm covers on her bed filled her mind.

"Why don't we go to my room? It has a fireplace."

Adler looked puzzled. "The students' rooms don't have fire-places." He took a moment to think it over. "Where is your room?"

Dihni smiled. "Do you want to find out?"

Adler hesitated. "Only because I'm freezing."

In Truest Form

As she wound her way through the corridors, Adler asked her where they were going. Normally, all the girls were in the student wings in the western corridors facing the south, and the boys were facing the north. Dihni's room was in the abandoned north end of the castle. Knowing every part of the castle, every nook, every secret passageway was an advantage to this setup.

She looked back at Adler, his face was ashen, and he looked a little skittish.

"There is no one and nothing in this part of the castle except for animals and plants. Old furniture and paintings are still in some rooms and halls. I know people say this part of the castle is haunted, but it isn't. It's lonely because this was the queen's part of the castle. When she died, King Eldornon forbade anyone from coming here. The servants would tell stories of seeing shadows and hearing the noises of someone living in these abandoned halls. There is a rumor that the queen died giving birth and that the doctor proclaimed the child had also died. It is said that the child lived and has roamed this part of the castle ever since."

Adler had been silent the whole time, and he chose now to speak. "But that was hundreds of years ago."

Dihni sighed. "Two hundred and thirty-six years ago, on December 13, to be exact."

Adler looked at her incredulously. "How do you know that?"

Dihni shrugged. "I know the history of this castle better than most."

Adler tried to get her to tell him more, but Dihni refused. Not another word was uttered. Dihni was impressed by his persistence because he wouldn't stop questioning her until she turned sharply, facing him fully, and gave him a look that clearly said, *shut up*.

As they went deeper into the queen's chambers, the abandoned feelings became stronger. For not even past the first three corridors would the robbers go. There were tattered drapes and curtains on the windows. Furniture was in pieces around the halls. Broken mirrors lay on the floor, the glass scattered across the floor. Pictures hung on the walls covered in dust so thick you could not see the photos underneath.

Dihni did not care to look at anything for she knew what lay before her as well as she knew the back of her own hand. Adler, however, gawked at everything.

When finally they came to the double doors that led into the queen's chambers, Adler stopped.

"Please don't tell me you sleep in the queen's chambers."

Dihni laughed. "No." Adler looked relieved. "I sleep in the tower."

At that, Adler blanched. Dihni squeezed his hand and chuckled.

Producing a silver key from her pocket, she then opened one of the double doors into the room that held what was left of the queen's magnificent rooms.

Dihni looked at nothing and walked over to a tapestry that was hung against the far-right wall. She lifted the side closest to the corner of the room and reached for the door that led to a staircase that went to the top of the tower where Dihni had made her bedroom.

Looking back for Adler, she found him standing in the doorway looking at the bed.

He looked like he had seen a ghost. She went up to him and put her hand on his arm. He jumped and looked down at her.

"This is where she died, isn't it?"

Dihni only nodded.

His face set, he nodded and walked with her to the tapestry.

Producing another, smaller, gold key, she unlocked the tower door. When she opened the door and went in, he gulped.

Looking back, she said, "Close the door."

He did and then followed her up.

As they walked up to the top of the tower, Dihni welcomed the silence. Even though it was awkward to share the silence of her tower with another person, she welcomed the company. It was high time she was not lonely anymore.

The tower door soon came into view. The dark wood was elegantly carved and had a big brass handle. Unlike the rest of the tower and castle doors, this door was trimmed with wood of a rich chestnut and mahogany color, as was the door a stunning contrast to the stone walls. It was Dihni's favorite part of her room, other than the fireplace wish was made of marble the color of pearls.

Dihni paused as she reached for the door handle, then looked at Adler.

"No one but me has been where you have now been. Remember that."

With that, she opened her door and stood aside so he could see inside. Adler gasped and walked into the room as if in a haze.

There was a gargantuan window on the east side that let morning light in. Under it was a wooden bench that was more of a flat top chest. Thick, heavy, dark-red velvet curtains were drawn back from the window with rope ties. A bed with sheer white curtains was across the room from the window on the west south curve of the chamber. An old wooden chest sat at the foot of the bed. The bed's posts and frame were polished wood of a dark cherry stain. Curtain rods went all the way around the top so that the curtains could be pulled closed. They were closed now.

Against the west curve of the walls was a table. It was a round masterpiece of wood carved elegantly, large enough for three people to dine and study at. Three chairs were set around it. A massive bookshelf built into the wall was filled with books of all kind and dominated most of the north wall. The stone made for an interesting-looking bookshelf. Its stone, just as aged as the rest of the castle, had a beige tint to it.

Between the shelf and the table was the fireplace with a screen of curving wrought iron metal pieces in front of the actual screen of chain mail. Over the mantel was a picture of the queen and the king. A vase of white flowers that bordered on pink were set on the right side of the picture, on the left a stand of a rosemary candle in honor of her memory. All shapes and sizes of candles lined the room. Some were on the windowsill, others on the table, even a few on the bookshelf. All of them with pools of wax dripping toward the floor.

The most astonishing thing about the room was that crawling vines blooming light-blue flowers streaked with white were growing from a small pot on the windowsill and had crawled over the walls making their way over the ceiling. Half the ceiling was already covered, and it had a few vines reaching over the bookshelf. Some of the oldest books, and the most precious that were rarely looked at for fear of damage, were being nestled in place by the vine as if it were protecting them from careless hands.

Adler wandered around the room touching the bed, the table, and then the bookshelf.

"These are so old!" He looked back at Dihni for a moment. "Did you find these in the castle?"

Dihni walked forward, closing the door behind her. "Yes. They are what is left of the royal library and the queen's personal collection."

Walking to the fireplace, she took a match and lit the fire. The wood and starter were already prepared, so Dihni need only strike the match and set it under the wood to start the flames.

Adler looked back at the books. He took one out and carefully opened it. Dihni reached for the book and gently took it out of his hands, putting it back on the shelf with the utmost care.

"They are not only old, Adler, but they are also very delicate."

He put his hand over her hand that was over the book and asked, "How long have you been here? Why couldn't I find your name in the schools' records? Why are you in this tower? What happened to you to make you shut yourself out?"

Dihni took a deep breath, still looking at the books. "For that, you have to sit down. This is a long story. You may not believe me. Just know that I am not something evil."

Adler looked at her with an expression of sympathy, curiosity, and wariness. When she made no attempt to move, he walked to the table. The chair legs whooshed across the ornate circular wool rug. He then sat down and waited patiently.

Dihni didn't know where to start. Many long minutes of silence passed until she finally decided on a proper opening.

"In answer to your questions," another pause of reflection, "I have been here for 236 years. You could not find me in the academy's register because you were looking at the wrong records. To find my name in congruence to this academy, you would have to look for the alias name I used when I founded this academy. I'm in this tower because I am free here. I can be who I am without having to worry about people finding me. I have stayed here most of my life. As for what happened to make me 'Shut myself out' as you put it, a lot of things." She turned to Adler, who looked stricken.

"Listen, and listen well, Adler Gilfni, for what you are about to hear not a soul has heard."

The Tales of Old

Dihni proceeded to tell him of how on the backsteps of the palace where the doctor had left her as the king had commanded a kitchen servant found Dihni as she was taking breakfast scraps to feed the pigs.

To her father, she was nothing more than trash, the reason his beloved queen had died.

Dihni told him of how the servant was full of compassion and decided to care for Dihni as her own. She realized that if the little princess was discovered and the king found out, Dihni would be taken and possibly killed. The woman kept Dihni safe and secret, teaching her to read and write, to do math, and the sciences. The servant was named Eniha. She was beautiful, with her golden skin, long dark hair, silver eyes, and slim frame.

When Dihni turned twenty and stopped aging, Eniha became curious and warry as did Dihni. After many years passed, and Dihni continued to show no signs of aging, Eniha and Dihni became obsessed with the strange phenomenon and decided to go to the queen's chambers. There they discovered behind a small picture of her when she was young a journal written in the queen's own hand. The first page contained a message. It read as thus, *Baby royal, this journal is for you so that you may know your ancestry and know who and what you are. I love you, dear one, be of good courage, faith, and happiness. You are not alone.*

The journal held the legacy of her mother's side of the family. It held the secrets of her kind. Her mother was no ordinary being; her mother was of an ancient race. They were called Kelie.

Kelie were a people of grace. They were the basis of the stories of the elves. The elves are a magical race, immortal, filled with powers, incredibly strong despite their lean, muscular, graceful dancer like forms. Kelie were not magical nor were they incredibly strong. They merely had a longer lifespan and were only stronger than the strongest human on earth.

The journal explained why Dihni had vision when miles ahead of her, she could see as perfectly as if she were standing there. Explaining how her Kelie blood made her stronger than everyone else, exceptionally graceful, have hearing that was so strong she could hear skin flaking off a person's body, and why her skin never blemished, and she never fell ill. It also explained why the Kelie had brighter or unnatural-colored eyes, and pale skin that seemed to glow in the sunlight.

At this point, Adler was sitting back in his chair with a calm and patient expression held on his face. At first, Adler had been shocked and appalled, and then when she came to explain about her race, he leaned back and simply listened as if he knew all too well the truths that Dihni was telling him.

She then went on to describe the biggest events throughout her life. She told him of how she had kept her people alive and well by being a "Robin Hood," stealing from the rich and giving to the poor. Dihni stopped rapists, murderers, thieves, men who beat on women and children. She settled many disputes between groups of traders, soldiers, commoners, wealthy nobles. Many of them were men and women in power, the people who claimed to be running the kingdom. They all called her "Mother of the People," or "Theno Opelet."

Dihni then spent much of her time learning from great teachers. There was a woman who taught her how to dance and control her movements. A man who taught her how to survive, how to use a bow and how to use it to hunt, how to use a sword, how to fight with only her body and her surroundings. There was also a couple who taught her how to run a household and how to cook and bake.

As she was learning all she could from her teachers, she realized just how much she loved knowledge and how it gave her freedom. She wanted to share that feeling. It filled her to the very brim, pooling over to people around her who would listen. But it wasn't enough, she needed to teach more people. That's when she revived her abandoned castle after the convergence and made it into an academy.

Dihni taught students for many years, but everyone started to notice how she never aged. Women and men alike came up to her and asked what her secret was. They asked how old she really was. They asked her all the questions she couldn't answer. So she left it up to the teachers to teach the students.

No longer would she teach self-defense and survival skills. She wouldn't ride with the students and teach them how to work with their horses. Her swordsmanship would not be used to teach others how to wield the deadly weapon.

However, Dihni could not stay on the sidelines and watch from the shadows. What could she do? She couldn't be the strange person running around the school, nothing more than a myth. Although that would be fun. No, she would have to become a student. That way, she could still help, but her looks would not be suspicious.

Dihni made it clear to Adler that she still ran the school, but none of the teachers knew who ran it; all they knew was that they got paid handsomely, taught students, and were given lavish living accommodations.

"I have been here for many years, running the academy. I plan on staying here. After one hundred years of educating myself in other parts of the world, I missed home. My hearts yearning was to come home and revive the love and joy that once filled the halls."

Adler sat with a thoughtful expression on his face. Dihni couldn't take. Getting up, she went to the window, looking out at the garden below. She wrapped her arms around herself, and despite the warm temperature of the room, she shivered.

Then a pair of arms wrapped around her and held her close to the body they were connected to.

Adler said softly, "You've been through a lot. Do you think you are alone, Dihni? Is that the real reason you shut yourself away?"

A single tear ran down Dihni's cheek. "I know I am alone." Her speech faltered. "At least, I thought I was. Then I saw you."

She turned and faced him. "No one has skin as pale as opal. No one has green eyes as bright as yours. Why didn't you come to me sooner? I've been completely alone while surrounded by people!" She whipped around and couldn't decide if she was angrier than hurt or just plain old furious.

Adler stood next to her. "I just got here last year, and you know this. I thought I was alone as well. Then I saw you. I was afraid to reveal myself. I wanted to badly, it tore me up. Sometimes I was inches away from you. I wanted to tell you, know you, and be with you but …" he trailed off into a silence that radiated sadness.

Dihni looked up and out the window, watching the sun descend and paint the sky pink and purple. After a moment, she said, "Tell me everything."

He began to tell his story.

He told of his father who had been a carpenter. His father had been a tall man with a strong build. He towered at least a foot over some of the other men in the village, all dark hair, tan skin, rough hands, and silver eyes. Despite his burly, rough appearance, Alder's father was quite gentle and kind, wise as an elder, and patient beyond his years.

Adler had worked with his father until the day he died. They made cabinets, chairs, cradles, beds, buckets for the well, tables, carts, coffins, most anything the village happened to need. And everything was beautiful with carvings that told a favorite story of the owners, or a fairytale, or something about the person.

His mother had been a seamstress. She had made all of the family's clothes and many other things. Blankets, gilts, gowns for all the women and girls, pants and shirts for the men and boys. Most of them were made out of wool that was weaved in the village, the finer clothes she used for special blankets and clothes that she sold in the market.

They both died around the same time. His mother had been murdered by robbers stealing her goods and clothes. When they saw her, they took her unnatural appearance as a sign that she was a witch and killed her without thought.

His father had hunted them down, and when he finally found them, he killed all of them. He was ready to leave and was about to do so, but before one of them died, he plunged a small dagger into his father's chest. His father had tried to make his way home but died by the river where Adler found him the morning after when he went looking for him after he had not come home that night.

After working his father's carpentry shop and training an apprentice, he left the shop and worked as a blacksmith's apprentice in the next village over for thirteen years. His mentor, a grumpy man but kind all the same, knew that Adler was different but didn't press him to divulge his secrets.

When he had finished his apprenticeship, he was then commissioned as a soldier for King Eldornon. He fought in all the greatest battles and a few of the smaller ones, quickly rising in rank from simple foot soldier to captain.

The soldiers looked up to him because he was a man that was filled with wisdom and only risked his men's lives if he knew and believed victory was at hand. They defeated many foes with the wisdom of Adler, who became renowned in the world for his successes.

It still haunted him today, all the faces of the men he had killed. Men who had pleaded for the sake of their families that he did not kill them. Boys who were no older than seventeen, sometimes younger who had screamed and tried to run from battle.

Adler's face clouded over, and he seemed to be haunted by the visions in his head. He shook his head as if to rid it of something and continued.

After the wars were over, he searched and searched for something to help him come to terms with the gruesomeness of the war, the cruelness of fight or die. He needed to find peace from what he had done and from the guilt and shame that overtook him.

Eventually, a wise old man came to him seemingly out of nowhere when Adler was in a drunken stupor wandering his way down the streets. After getting Adler sober and back to the picture of health, the man taught him how to survive in the wilderness, much like Dihni's teacher.

Adler told her of another teacher who had taught him the ways of music. How it flowed out of a person and brought about emotions buried within.

Dihni smiled, maybe they were much more alike than they realized.

He was taught many of the same things that she was taught: survival tactics, music, the ability to use weapons.

It pleased her to think that he was a lot like her. It just meant another piece connected them other than the fact that they were of the same race. Another little bit of loneliness faded away and her spirits rose.

After he was done with his lessons and his teachers had long since passed away, he traveled the world. He lived off the many abilities he had gained from his years of teachings, working with gypsies, blacksmiths, hunters, merchants, farmers, and exploring the land.

Adler traveled to Scotland, Ireland, India, America, and Japan. Everywhere he went was wonderful, exhilarating, and fun, yet all that he saw could never fill his heart with joy like his homeland in England did.

He came back home and heard rumors about an academy. People said that the academy did not have a dean and no one knew who ran the school. He asked people who the dean had been before and no one could answer him. It seemed as if the school ran itself. Teachers occasionally got letters from whoever ran the school and said that the letters were written with what seemed to be a quill pen and sealed with wax.

In trying to find out more about the mysterious dean, he searched all the history records for anything on the school. He found out that the academy was actually the old castle he had once lived in for a short time when he was a foot soldier. The founder of the academy was a woman who went missing after years of teaching students herself.

That's when he saw Dihni. Just by looking at her once, he knew what she was but didn't know who. He had been trying to learn more about her ever since and couldn't stand it anymore. He had to meet her.

"When I saw you up on that bridge, I knew that I had to stop you. I knew that if you left me in this world, I would have to die because my heart would shrivel up."

Adler had his hand against her cheek, cradling her face. He had to constantly wipe away her tears.

Dihni never looked away from his eyes. So she saw his emotions whirling around. She saw him lean down. And she did nothing to stop him.

When his lips touched hers it was a soft, tentative, gentle kiss. Yet it carried a shock wave with it.

They both gasped at the same time.

Adler breathlessly said, "I thought finding your shock mate, your Ohet Ma, was a myth."

Dihni whispered, "Apparently not."

They collided with such passion, love, and understanding that it seemed impossible to pull apart.

Adler picked her up, and Dihni wrapped her legs around his waist. One of his hands was in her hair and the other on her back. He stumbled across the room. His toe hit the end of her bed, and he slowly bent down and laid her on it.

He pulled away and looked into her eyes. Dihni answered the question in his eyes by starting to pull his jacket off. He stood and took it off, dropping it on the floor.

Dihni sat up and kissed him. Adler put his hands on her hips and slid her shirt up. She raised her arms as he pulled it off.

His eyes wandered over her for a moment and then looked back into her eyes. He ripped off his shirt and came closer to her.

Laying her back with their lips connecting over and over again, he pulled her up to the top of the bed. Dihni kicked off her shoes. Adler then undid the belt and button of her jeans. He started to tug them down, but Dihni sat up and stopped him by undoing his belt and button.

He smiled. "Me first? That's not how it goes, little lady."

Dihni smiled. "Ah, but his belt and button are always first. Then the little ladies."

Adler chuckled. "Fine then, Your Highness."

Dihni hit him, and he retaliated by swiftly stepping off the bed and taking her pants with him. He then rushed at her, somehow leaving his pants behind as well.

He undid her bra and slid it off, kissing her neck and shoulders. Then he moved down. Dihni gasped, not only were his lips wandering but his hands as well.

He sat up and ripped the fabric that was around her, throwing the tattered garment away.

He stood and took off his own last garment. He knelt back down on the bed. He kissed every part of her body that his lips could reach, paying attention to certain areas more than others.

Dihni repaid the favor in kind. Then he pulled her up and kissed her, laying her on her back. He positioned himself over her, and with one final action, sealed their bond for life.

The rest of the night was spent in a torrent of passion.

It was well into the night, and it was as if only an hour had passed. The sky was starting to lighten when they finally collapsed, utterly spent.

The only thing Dihni felt was her racing heartbeat and the heat that was rushing through her body. It was as though her limbs were phantoms. She was acutely aware of them, but they were so tired that they ceased to exist.

After the Storm

Long after the sun had risen and shone through Dihni's window, they were still fast asleep.

Until Dihni slowly woke from the dreamworld. Being half asleep, she cuddled against the warm body next to her, wishing to go back to sleep and stay snuggly warm. However, her efforts were futile.

As soon as she opened her eyes and looked upon Adler, memories of the night before filled her mind immediately. A sigh of complete and utter satisfaction sounded forth from her puffy lips. Looking up at the curtain tent around them, she wondered at how beautiful everything looked this morning and then looked at Adler.

She gazed at him in his sleep with such love she thought she might burst. Dihni swept her fingers across his forehead and moved the hair out of his face. Propping herself up on her elbow just to look at his peaceful face.

Adler opened his eyes, and the sight before him made him smile. Dihni was above him, and the sun shone through her hair, creating a halo of curls, her smiling face glowing above him.

She was, he thought, the most beautiful vision.

He reached up and touched her face.

Dihni bent down and kissed him lightly. "Good morning"

"I'm going to wake up with you next to me for the rest of our lives," Adler said it with such love and compassion it made Dihni melt and warm up all over.

"You are my Ohet Ma, Adler Gilfni."

Adler sat up, his hand on the back of her neck, easing her back on the bed. Dihni lay down all the way.

"And you are mine, Dihni Nednepe."

He kissed her forehead and then lay back down, stroking her arm.

Dihni smiled and sighed again, perfectly content.

Just then, they heard a splash.

They looked at each other, a question clearly written on their faces, *What was that?*

The splash sounded again and, with it, the sound of a woman's voice calling for Dihni.

Adler and Dihni jumped out of bed and put on their clothes. They were in such a rush that they put on the clothes they had been previously wearing the day before.

Dihni relinquished getting another pair of undergarments, however, because Adler had ripped her other ones, and there wasn't time.

Dihni grabbed her keys and ran for the door. Adler was in front of her. He ran down the stairs and opened the door at the bottom while she closed and locked the bedroom door.

Dihni ran down the stairs and jumped through the tower door, slamming it closed, and locking it as fast as she could.

Adler and Dihni ran through the halls and corridors of the castle. Students were roaming about the grounds. It appeared as though they did not hear or see anything.

There were two places the splash could have come from. There was the outdoor pool that the students and staff used, and there was the lake-sized pond in the center of the maze.

They ran past the still waters of the pool just to be sure that the sound hadn't come from there. It was obvious that it hadn't.

They continued on to the maze. Dihni didn't want to take the time to navigate through the maze so she jumped on top of the hedges. Looking over, she saw Adler jump up with her. He gained his balance, nodded at her, and they bounded over the hedges toward the center garden.

The hedges were thick and sturdy. They did not move as Adler and Dihni leaped on them.

As they neared the garden, it was clear something was going on. The birds were screaming and flapping around as if something unwanted was in the garden. Trees were shaking, their leaves fluttering to the ground.

The garden was in chaos.

Screaming birds and shaking trees didn't faze Dihni. What did shock her was the woman in the lake. Her hair was dark and long, braided far past what Dihni could see. The woman's skin was pale and shimmery. Not the kind of shimmer that Dihni and Adler had, but more of a dewy, water-logged shimmer.

The mark of sea magic.

She was waving both arms frantically, periodically diving to slap her mottled green tale against the water.

They reached the last hedge and jumped off it, landing by the water. The water nixie swam up to them breathless and wide-eyed. Her long hair was decorated with shells and braids, lips smooth and shimmered with gold, eyelids a pale pink that brought out the bright-gold color of her eyes, high cheekbones, and a perfectly set jaw. She was breathtaking.

"I have news for you, Princess."

Dihni flinched at the formal title. The nixie took no notice of her reaction, for this nixie was not panicked but ecstatic.

Dihni looked around at the garden and saw that the chaos was, in fact, the birds singing and dancing. Were the trees moving?

The nixie looked at Adler astonished. "You don't know the legend? I thought for sure that you would." She looked at Dihni. "Did not your mother leave you the story of the legend?"

Dihni started at the mention of her mother. "She left me a journal, but it said nothing of a legend."

The nixie looked confused. "Your mother would not have left you in the dark. She must have left it for you somewhere only you would be able to find it. Perhaps in an old book or locked chest of some sort. She was very clever."

With a sharp look up at the nixie's face, Dihni looked deep into her eyes. "Did you know my mother?"

The nixie looked at Dihni with sadness, her eyes shimmering. "Yes, I knew your mother very well."

The Legend

Dihni started to ask her about her mother, but the water nixie interrupted her. "I'm sorry, but we do not have time. I must tell you the legend, and then we should be off."

Dihni nodded, a little sad, but knowing there were more important things.

The once-great people of the Kelie were almost wiped out of existence. During the great wars of the human race, they fled so deep into their kingdom that they were left unallied. All their trade routes with the human world were cut off, and they began to starve for their crops were not bearing enough food.

Men, women, and children began dying from sickness and starvation. The people begged their king and queen to help, but they were just as starved and sick as their people and could not help, save but send them into the world to keep them from extinction.

The surviving Kelie fled to try to survive and rebuild their great race. A few of them decided to blend with the mortals and give them strength among their people. It was not a popular decision.

Dihni and Alder both started at this bit of information, but the nixie took no notice and continued her story.

"But the Kelie race has become too diluted and sparse. You must all come together and rebuild. A portal has been opened in this garden so that I could come to you and take you to your rightful kingdom."

"That's what caused the garden to fright, wasn't it?"

The nixie nodded. "Yes."

Dihni shivered. She had felt as though something were different this morning.

She turned to the water nixie. "There is still one more thing I do not understand. What do we have to do with this?"

The nixie took their hands. "We need every being with Kelie blood once more. Without all of you, it is unlikely the race will survive."

Adler and Dihni looked at each other in confusion and disbelief.

Dihni turned to the nixie. "Where are the others?"

The nixie squeezed her hand. "I'm going to take you to them now."

With that, she pulled them into the water and deep into the depths of the pool. It was dark and cold, but a small light ahead of them was visible. As they swam closer, the light grew, and soon it consumed them. Dihni covered her eyes, and when the light faded and they started swimming up, she uncovered them.

They could not see anything above the surface of the water, but it was clear that they were not at the academy anymore. The only light they could see was a golden orange that was clearly from a fire from the way it danced and flickered.

The ever-nearing surface brought muffled noise with it that sounded like many people gathering together. When they breached the surface, the noise of hundreds of people talking, cheering, and guffawing berated them with a background of music.

"Hey, look there, in the pool!" someone shouted.

"Have a nice swim?" someone else asked.

Everyone around the so-called pool laughed.

It was indeed a small pool of water surrounded by rocks that gradually became larger around the back, where they had just come from.

The people around the pool were wearing clothes from all over the world, but all of them had a few things in common, bright eyes, pale skin.

Kelie people, hundreds of them.

Dihni was confounded—mouth open, eyes wide, stunned look, confounded.

A man crouched at the edge of the pool. He had long wavy brown hair and violet eyes. He was striking.

"Are you going to take my hand, or is there a tail under there that your hiding?"

He never lost his smile even though Dihni scowled at him.

"Now, Baron, be nice, unlike you, she's an outsider. However, unlike her, I will be needing your help out of here." The nixie chuckled as she helped Dihni and Adler out of the pool.

Once they were out, she grabbed Baron's hand, and he pulled her out of the water and held her to him.

"What are the magic words?" he teased.

The nixie grinned. "If you put me down, you might get a dance, and a kiss."

Baron chuckled. "Now how can I say no to that?"

With that, he kissed her and set her on the grass. As soon as her fins touched the grass, her tail began to transform into legs. When the transformation was complete, she was left barefoot, wearing a silken skirt the colors of her tail, leaning into Baron.

Adler awkwardly cleared his throat.

The couple jumped, and Adler chuckled.

"I take it you too know each other."

Nixie smoothed her skirt while Baron held out his hand to Adler.

"The name's Baron, this is my wife, Ilia. Hope you don't mind a little smooching now and then because I can't help it ..." He leaned into Adler. "And neither can she."

He nudged Adler with his elbow and laughed. Then he turned to Dihni. "And this lovely lady must be yours." He took Dihni's hand and kissed the top of it. "Charmed. What's your name?"

Dihni stood there in shock. This was a culture shock she was not prepared for. People, like her, were everywhere, and one of them was married to a water nixie. It was too much.

Dihni was so deep into her shock that she didn't notice that Adler spoke for her.

"This is Dihni, she's a bit in shock from all this." He gestured to the giant group of Kelie people and then to Baron and Ilia. "Is there somewhere we can get away and get changed perhaps?"

Ilia stepped forward. "Of course, I'll take you to your rooms." She paused. "Oh wait, I'm guessing you'll want a room together?"

Dihni spoke up, "Yes, please." She put her hand to her mouth. The voice that came from her was panicked and desperate.

Everyone looked at her with sympathetic smiles. Ilia stepped forward and put her hands on Dihni's shoulders. And when she looked into the golden depths of her eyes, Dihni calmed extensively.

"Now, how about we get you to your room and dry you off?"

Ilia put her arm around Dihni and led her away from the pool. They walked through and around people, then around a bonfire that was nearly as big as her.

When they finally rounded the fire, what stood before them resonated within their beings a sense of awe. Houses were built around the trees, encircling them. As they walked closer, it became clear that the houses were not separated from the trees, but rather they were the trees.

Ilia laughed. "It's old magic. The trees' trunks were shaped into houses that will grow. Really quite simple actually."

With a bit more than a hint of curiosity, Adler asked, "When you said we get a room …?" He gestured to the tree houses.

Ilia smiled. "No, you two are staying somewhere else. Somewhere very special."

As they wove their way through the earthen streets, it became clear that there was no actual planned out method for where these houses were placed. They were where the trees had decided to grow with regular trees in between.

And then the trees opened and there, nestled in what would have been a clearing was a glorious tree castle. The trees from around the clearing grew so that they enveloped it like a protective shell. The roof had long since branched out and grown more trees atop it: beautiful evergreens, maples, willow trees, and what looked to be blossom trees that might bear fruit.

It was breathtaking.

Ilia stood patiently waiting for them to take it in; however, Baron wasn't so patient.

"Okay! Let's get this train back on the tracks and go inside." He side-hopped toward the double doors and gestured with a shoving motion.

Ilia chuckled and Dihni was eager to get out of her cold wet clothes that clung to her in a very uncomfortable way.

Castle Memories

As they walked through the castle's smooth double doors, warmth and comfort seeped into their very souls. The rich browns and reds of the wood oozed with it, and the autumn colors of the decor and furniture brought it to life. Here and there, a spot of white or blue took those autumn colors and comfort and gave them a sense of joy.

It was breathtaking.

Then Baron jumped in front of them. "As you can see by the ginormous fireplace, couches, chairs, and tables, this is the living room of the castle. Down the hall toward your right, you will find the throne room, library, and other various rooms, including a ballroom. Down the hall towards your left, you will find the kitchen, dining hall, and none of the other rooms really matter. Now, if you will follow me."

Baron pivoted on one foot and walked into the living room. When you walk in, you notice a crackling fire that was indeed large on the left, and on the right a gargantuan bookshelf with rolling ladders. The bookshelf sat under a set of wide stairs leading up to the second floor. The banisters were growing vines with purple flowers on them that drooped and crawled atop the highest books on the shelf. When the staircase reached the second level, the hall continued around, above the fire place, and back to the staircase. The same banister with cascading flower vines went all the way around in a never-ending growth loop. Everything blended together with perfect balance and never a sharp corner, even the edges of the stairs were smooth and rounded.

As they reached the top of the stairs, Baron began to speak again. "The second floor are all bedrooms and studies. King and queen's chambers are on the right, along with esteemed guest rooms. Servant and other guest rooms are on the left, including your room, which we will take you to now because if I do any more showing around, you will freeze, and my wife will get mad at me. Happy wife, happy life! Right, honey?"

Ilia smiled and shook her head, amused at her husband's statement.

"You are practically bouncing with anticipation. Ever since you mentioned the kitchen, you haven't stopped thinking about it. Go taste testing, I'll take care of them."

Baron jumped and whooped pumping his fist in the air. He gave Ilia a kiss and ran down the stairs and off to the kitchen.

Ilia beckoned them to follow her down the left corridor. "Now, just because your room is not in the right wing does not mean it won't be beautiful or luxurious. These rooms come with a full bathroom, half the size of the bedroom, and a sitting room. Here we are!"

She stopped in front of a door with a peacock carved on it and handed them a key with a blue ribbon on it.

"You two get warm and wash up. Your clothes will be waiting for you on the bed when you get out. If the maids have done their job, a hot bath should already be waiting for you. When you're done, feel free to come down to the kitchen and eat. Something tells me you'll not be coming back to the party."

She turned to go back toward the kitchen to find her husband.

"Wait! How will we know what to do in the morning? Will you come back and get us?" Adler called.

Ilia called from over her shoulder. "Come down to the lobby in the morning, we'll meet you there."

Adler unlocked the door to reveal a room filled with colors.

After a moment, he said, "Well, I guess we know why there's a peacock on the door."

He looked down at Dihni smiling, only to see her huddled and shivering with an exhausted look on her face. His smiled became sympathetic and he pulled her into a hug.

"Let's get in that bath."

Adler led them into the room and shut the door behind them.

The sitting room was filled with blues, yellows, greens, black, white, and purple hues. There were two chairs and a slipper couch situated in front of a small fireplace. All of them made with a blue fabric embroidered with yellow and green patterns. A small piano was across the room on the right. Large windows straight across from the door were covered by dark-purple curtains with tassels on the ends.

Two doors were on either side of the room. Adler looked from one to the other. "You go to the one on the left, and I'll go to the one on the right."

Dihni shuffled her way to the door on the right, trying not to move too much to avoid the awkward rubbing of her clothes.

When she opened the door all efforts to remain slightly comfortable vanished like the steam that was gently rising from the bathtub. Dihni dropped the towel around her shoulders and started ripping her clothes off.

When she reached the tub, she put her foot in and half gasped, half shrieked. The hot water made her frozen toes tingle. She sat down and lay back breathing deeply because the tingly feeling was everywhere. Dihni closed her eyes and let her body relax.

"I can't recall ever seeing you so relaxed."

Dihni felt the water shift as Adler got in the large tub.

"You are so relaxed that if I sang, you'd fall asleep. Now, can you please come over here?"

Dihni opened her eyes to find Adler lounging against the end of the tub. She grabbed the edges of the tub and slid over to him, straddling his lap. He put his hands on her hips and gently pulled her down, kissing her chest, then her collarbone, and up her neck.

It was an odd sensation in the tub, but neither one of them was willing to stop. A while later, curled up on top of Adler, Dihni realized that the water had cooled off and was no longer creating a tingly feeling.

Not wanting to get cold again, she made her way out of the tub and found a couple of towels; wrapping herself up, she walked back to Adler and handed him the towel.

He smiled up at her dreamily and took the towel still lying in the tub. "I think I'm too exhausted to move."

Dihni smiled back at him. "Well, when you find the energy, I'll be waiting for you in the kitchen. I don't know about you, but I'm starving."

Making her way through the sitting room toward the bedroom door, Dihni heard the water sloshing in the tub. She opened the door to the bedroom, unsurprised to find that is was made in the same colors as the sitting room and bathroom.

The bed was in a canopy style with see-through dark-purple curtains that shone like sunlight on a glassy expanse of water and felt like silk. The bedspread was blue with purple patterns on it. At the foot of it, there was a chest stained a dark chestnut and decorated with a gold clasp. Dihni wondered if it was for personal effects and shoes perhaps.

On the other side of the room was an armoire with a place to hang coats and drawers for clothing. Dihni went to it and found two different sizes of coats and boots. The top drawer was filled with pants, shirts, and socks for Adler. In the second drawer were similar garments save a few. Dihni found a soft leather corset and was delighted to see it there, hers had frayed and ripped long ago.

On the bed were two sets of clothes, on one set was a similar corset. Dihni placed the other corset in the drawer and turned toward the clothes laid out for her. Dihni put on the cotton undergarments and promptly took off the bottom set. A few hours without them, and she found she no longer wanted them.

She then proceeded to put on the shirt. It was soft and flowing, the medium tone of blue brought out the shine in her pale skin. The sleeves were loose and gathered at the wrists; the collar similarly gathered, but loose. There were ties that could be used to gather it more; Dihni cinched it a bit, leaving it loose. She then pulled on the fitted pants, unsure of what they were made of. Dihni made a mental note to ask Ilia later.

Finally, she put on the soft leather corset and pulled at the ties until it fit snugly but didn't restrict her in any way. The corset was more of a big leather strap than an actual corset, much like something you would see a pirate wench wearing. They were the ones that made them popular after all.

From the doorway, an intake of breath made Dihni pause her dressing and turn.

Standing in the door was a flushed wet towel wrapped Adler with a stunned look upon his face.

With a deep chuckle Dihni asked, "Is there something wrong with my outfit?"

Adler walked up to her and roughly yanked her to him. "Absolutely not."

There was a hungry look upon his face, and Dihni knew exactly what he was thinking. "Adler, I'm starving, I need food. Get dressed, and when you're ready, come down to the kitchen."

Unfortunately, Dihni's shoes were still dripping wet, so she took the ankle-high leather lace-ups at the foot of the bed.

"Dihni, you forgot your socks."

Adler was holding a pair of white cotton socks. "Did you notice these clothes are all either leather or cotton?"

Dihni nodded, energy was quickly draining to a trickle, and she needed food badly. She laced up her boots, stood, gave Adler a kiss, and left their rooms.

Turning toward the stairs, Dihni didn't bother to look around, but instead made her way down the stairs and back to the front door. Baron had said the kitchen was down the left hallway, but he didn't say where in the hall.

Most castle kitchens were in the very last room at the end of the hallway. Considering the oddity of this castle, Dihni kept an eye out for kitchen doors and kept her nose open for smells. The hall was curved, and rooms were on either side, it seemed as though the castle was rounded both in and out.

Just as she was wondering if she would ever find the kitchen, there before stood two doors with no handles and big round windows. Inside, she could see long counters covered in flour and baking ingredients. Baron and Ilia were seated at one of them, eating what looked to be a couple of pies.

Dihni pushed open one of the doors and was hit by the fragrant warm. Her stomach growled, and her mouth watered with anticipation for food.

Baron and Ilia turned and laughed.

"Come over here and have some pie before that gets any louder," Baron said.

Ilia lifted a spoon and set it across the counter for her. Walking up to them, Dihni realized that one of the pies was a berry pie of some sort, and the other was a meat pie.

"Well, don't you look fetching," Ilia praised. "I do believe blue is your best color."

Baron was less interested in her clothes and more interested in the pies. "Check it out, dinner and dessert in the same form."

Dihni smiled. "This will be breakfast for me."

Baron swallowed the bite in his mouth. "Right, because you guys were awakened by this lovely creature."

Just as Ilia playfully slapped him on the shoulder Adler came through the kitchen doors. This time, Dihni was taken aback by his appearance.

He was wearing the same boots as Dihni's, black leather with lace-ups. His pants were also black and made from the same material as the pants Dihni wore, they weren't as fitted and left a bit of wiggle room. The shirt, however, was white and had a more open collar than hers; he didn't even tie the front or pull it at all. Instead, he had tucked it in. He had taken his belt from his old pants and in the belt loops of his new ones.

In his hand was his sopping jacket. As he lifted it, he said, "I may have left a drip trail, but I couldn't leave it. I was hoping there was a way to dry it. The fireplace in our room has nothing to start a fire."

Ilia pointed at a fireplace against the far wall. Dihni hadn't even noticed it before.

"Hang it in front of the fireplace. It should dry in a jiff."

Adler beamed and practically skipped over to the fireplace.

Turning back to the pies, Dihni was surprised to find a plate with a slice of meat pie on it as well as a slice of berry pie.

"Well, are you going to eat it, or stare at it?" Baron said as he put back the pie server for the sweet pie.

"Thank you. I think, I'll eat it."

Adler came back and settled himself next to Dihni as she took the first bite of her berry pie. She immediately forked another bite; this pie was blackberry pie, her absolute favorite.

"I think I need some of that pie." Adler chuckled.

"It's blackberry pie, cooks best in my opinion. Dihni's too, it looks like."

Dihni was on her fourth bite already and knew that she would have more after the meat pie. Meanwhile, Adler served himself up some pie and chatted with Ilia and Baron. Opting not to listen to the conversation and enjoy her food, Dihni quickly finished the sweet pie and moved on to the savory.

It looked to be some sort of light meat with potatoes, carrots, and other veggies, much like a chicken potpie. Taking a bite, she discovered it was in fact a chicken potpie, equally as delicious as the berry pie. It was put away in nearly the same time as the berry pie.

The others were still in deep conversation, and Dihni still wasn't listening. She reached for the blackberry pie server and made the mistake of glancing at the others. They were all smiling and chuckling at her. Dihni unapologetically put her second slice of berry pie on her plate.

Adler wrapped his right arm around her shoulders and squeezed her. "I have never seen you so excited about food."

Dihni acknowledged him with a kiss to the cheek and went back to her pie.

After finishing their lovely baked meal, Dihni and Adler strolled arm in arm through the halls back to their room. Baron and Ilia were right beside them hand in hand.

"Hey, Ilia, considering that we pretty much woke up only a few hours ago, why are we so tired?" Dihni said with a yawn.

"When we went through the portal in the pool, it created a similar effect as jet lag. The stress and unfamiliarity of everything can make anyone tired, especially when you're stuffed with good food."

At that, everyone laughed. They all had eaten more than one slice of pie. When they had finished, there was hardly any pie left.

Going back to their rooms, everyone said good night. Many others were in the hallways and living room saying good night, talking softly to each other. Adler took the room key out of his pocket and opened the door. Standing aside, he motioned for Dihni to go in. Dihni smiled and walked straight for the bedroom, not hesitating one bit. She took off all her clothes and crawled into the plush covers. The sheets were soft, and the blanket was thick and fluffy, filled to the brim with feathers. The pillows were equally plush but were not filled with feathers, as far as Dihni could tell.

Just as she was settling into the bed, Adler came through the door and laughed.

"You, my love, have not been waiting for me at all today."

Dihni could only make a single sigh and then a yawn as a response. Adler climbed into the bed, equally as devoid of clothes as her. Snuggling up against her, he kissed her forehead and said good night.

Dihni promptly fell asleep and dreamed that she was being smothered in a crowd of people. She had no idea where she was or what was happening. Her limbs would not obey her and her mind kept drifting. This was how her night unfurled itself.

Battles Beginning

The next morning, they awoke to the smell of eggs and bacon. On the table in their sitting room was a small breakfast feast. Eggs, bacon, bread, fruit, juice, and coffee were quickly devoured.

After they had eaten, they decided to get dressed and see if they could find Ilia and Baron. Instead of picking out new clothes, they put on what they had worn last night, seeing as they had only been worn for a few hours.

"These feel a lot less tight when you're not stuffed with pie." Adler chuckled as he put on his pants. Dihni laughed and agreed with him. They left their rooms and started making their way to the living room.

Just as they were rounding the corner to the top of the stairs, Baron came barreling into them.

With a jump and a yell, Baron stopped before there was a chance for a collision.

"Aah! You guys are late! Come on, hurry up before Ilia has a reason to bust my balls."

He turned and started to run down the stairs. Dihni and Adler simply looked at each other, utterly confused.

Baron popped around the corner. "Come on!"

Sensing his dire need, Adler and Dihni followed after him. Running down the stairs was annoying Dihni, and she vaulted herself over the railing, landing in front of a startled Baron, who stood there stunned.

"Are we not late for something?"

Baron pulled himself out of his stupor and started to run out the door again. "I can't believe you just did that."

He threw open the castle door and started beelining around a crowd of people. Adler and Dihni followed him to a table where Ilia and many others were seated.

"Hello, sleepyheads. Thank you, sweetheart, that took less time than I thought it would."

Adler and Dihni took the empty seats next to their friends.

"What exactly is going on here?" Adler asked.

"You'll see," Baron said, smiling as he climbed and stood on top of the table.

"Oi! Shut your gobs and listen up!"

Many of the people started to laugh, one even yelled at Baron asking why he got to stand on the tables and yell at them.

"I'll tell you why, because I live here, and you're a quest."

Very few people did not laugh at Baron's statement.

"Now I know you've all been wondering the exact reason why we're here. Well, I'll tell you, we're here because we are going to rebuild our civilization."

Many people nodded their heads and murmured agreement.

"What you didn't know was that all of you who were born of royal descent are in the running for the crowns of our fair ancestral queen and king! I have seated at this table the few who have royal blood and their spouses. They will compete against each other by trial. These will not be any ordinary trials by combat. No, these are going to test the character, strength, perseverance, and heart of each of these lucky few."

Turning so that he faced those seated at the table, he began informing them on what lay ahead.

"Royals, your trials will be to forge a weapon that represents who you are as a warrior. Go to the Dragons of Senna and hatch an egg to protect the kingdom. Finally, you must seek out the fairies of Andros and receive their magic as well. One last thing, your spouses may help you, but they must not participate. If someone who does not have royal blood helps in anything but the weapon forge, they will perish, or maybe just be eliminated. May you prevail and come out crowned!"

The crowd cheered and went back to their party with more vigor and excitement than before. However, not everyone at the table was as enthusiastic. Three women and two men got up from the table and approached Baron. They pulled him aside and had a heated conversation, from which he came back with a scowl upon his face.

He leaned against the table, one hand around a cup of what looked to be an ale or beer.

Ilia put her hand on his shoulder. "You cannot make all of them participate."

Baron took a deep breath and blew it out, which seemed to calm him. "Yes, but I do not like it when people cower from greatness just because the journey may be difficult."

Adler made a questioning gesture. "Excuse me, but what exactly just happened?"

Baron turned to him. "Those cowards just forfeit their claim to the throne. I knew some would, but it still irks me, and don't you two even think about it. There is something in you that is prime royal material.

An expression of curiosity came upon Baron's face just then, as though he had just thought of something he hadn't before. He looked at them and then shook his head.

"If you have something to ask us, then you would do well to ask," Dihni said impatiently. Being forced to be around all these people was making her irritable.

Baron smiled and sat back in his chair. "I was just thinking that you guys were probably in your nineties, and that's why I get the vibe you would be such great rulers." He chuckled and started to drink from his cup.

Dihni smiled and said, "I appreciate the compliment, but I'm actually about to turn two hundred and thirty-seven."

Baron choked and spewed his drink everywhere. Then he turned to Dihni mouth agape as he looked her up and down. Ilia slapped his arm, and he snapped out of his shaken state.

"You're telling me that you are in fact over two hundred years old? Adler, how old are you?"

Dihni stuttered for a bit, she hadn't even thought about asking how old he was. It shocked her that it had never come up.

Adler chuckled and answered, "I'll be nearing 242 in a few months."

Baron, absolutely flabbergasted, turned to his loving wife, who had a very amused expression upon her face. "Did you know how old they were?"

She laughed. "I knew how old Dihni was, seeing as I knew her mother when I was a young girl. However, I did not know Adler's age. Darling, don't look so shocked, being as old as you are."

Adler chuckled. "Hey, Baron, how old are you?"

Baron turned and looked sheepish, his face turning a bit pink. He mumbled an answer into his cup as he took a swig.

Adler laughed even more, and this time, Ilia and Dihni both chuckled a bit.

"Sorry, what was that? I didn't quite catch what you said."

Baron looked deeply into his cup and answered tersely, "Seventy-four," before taking another gulp of ale.

Instead of laughing, Adler and Dihni looked upon the odd couple with confused expressions.

Ilia nodded understanding the unspoken question. "In the water, time runs differently than above. I was unaware of the upper realm until your mother came to us. Back then, I was just a child. My age now is a mere sixty-seven. I prefer not to go by land years because I was not born here and even the mental aging here is different."

Dihni jolted back to remembering that Ilia knew her mother and suddenly acquired a longing to speak with her about the woman who had given her life.

She was about to ask Ilia if they could converse in private when someone interrupted them.

"Very interesting aging in your little group. Some might even say unnatural."

Standing before them was a man wearing a red shirt, black jeans, converse shoes, and a few bracelets. Something warned Dihni not to trust this man.

"With all due respect, the only *thing* unnatural here is an uninvited conversation."

His smirk slipped off his face, and his entire countenance hardened. "You would do well not to make enemies out of your competition, Princess. With all due respect, you may not survive the ordeal."

Dihni placed a hand upon the table and slowly rose so that they were inches away from each other. "May I remind you that you do not know me, and therefore, should not pertain to assume that I will be easy to defeat. There is more to a book than its cover."

His smirked returned. "Books are wonderful things, you can learn so much from them. However, there are always little bits of information on their sleeves."

The man stood straight and turned, then looking over his shoulder he said, "Till the next time, Princess."

Dihni felt a hand on her back gently easing her back into the chair. She didn't resist, but her eyes followed the red-shirted man as he made his way to talk to others.

"Baron, status report." She really didn't trust this man.

Adler gave a big-eyed look to Baron who was stuttering a bit. He cleared his throat and began telling them all about their unwelcome visitor. "His name is Kegan, he's from Japan. Very wealthy family, smart, strong, honor bound, and traditional values. Except his wardrobe, obviously he's a bit modern. Loves his power color too. Only a select few can stand him, and they're either part of his family, staff, or under his belt. Prince Kegan is not someone you want to cross, you just had to insult him."

Dihni huffed and looked at Baron and Ilia. "He insulted you first."

They smiled at her warmly, understanding that she was accepting them into her very small circle. Then Baron smiled even bigger and went back to his bouncy persona. "I just remembered you guys have to get to the forge and build your weapons in half an hour."

Baron stood. "All royal contestants will be expected at the weapons forge in half an hour! Do not be late!"

Then he looked at Dihni and Adler and motioned for them to follow him. Standing from the table, they all started walking away from the castle and the gathering of people.

Ilia had been rather quiet that morning but a bump from Baron got her to smile and tell them about the forge.

"The weapons forge is really a very interesting place. Unlike the castle and the houses, it's not made from a tree. They tried it once, and it did not go well, they ended up burning it down. So instead, they set everything outside and built a fence of sorts around it. It has everything a normal weaponry would have: anvils, water tubs, tools, fireplaces—you name it. It's not much farther away now, and if you ever feel the urge to come out here again, you won't get lost."

After a few minutes of silent walking through the woods, the trees simply ended. There was no gradual thinning or indications that the forestry would open up; instead there was a wall of thick bushes about eight feet in height. Ilia was right, there was no way they would ever not be able to find the forge.

Adler pointed at the wall of bushes. "How exactly are we supposed to get in? Is there an opening somewhere?"

Baron chuckled. "No, mate, there isn't an opening," he paused and gave them a knowing grin, "yet."

Then he stepped forward and whispered something into the bushes. The foliage sprang to life, and with the sound of rustling leaves and cracking branches, there was an archway before them.

Baron, who had been watching them the entire time, laughed and walked through the space in the bushes.

"You will learn how to open it if you complete all the trials and receive the crowns. For now, this will have to be open all day and probably into the night. Speaking of which, have you guys thought of your weapons that you will be making?"

Just as Dihni was about to answer, they passed through the thick wall of greenery and into a clearing unlike any she had seen.

There were three great woodburning fireplaces specifically made for heating metal. In front of the furnaces, there was an anvil with two buckets of water. Worktables followed the buckets, as well as grinding stones to sharpen the blades. On the left of them stood a collection of metals and molds for the weapons to form in. On the right of the workstations was a large collection of different woods, leathers, and fibers.

It was an expansive clearing, and there was no confusion on why it was such a special place. This was meant for people who could focus on their craft and be inspired.

"Pretty amazing, isn't it? You never answered my question by the way."

Dihni turned to him. "I was going to say that I wasn't sure yet. I've always used multiple weapons instead of relying on merely one. Any chance we're allowed more than one?"

Baron shook his head. "No. You are only allowed to make one weapon."

Dihni nodded and walked over to the metals. She ran her hand along them as she walked by. They were cold to the touch and hard. Then she went to the wood and ran her hand along them as well. Unlike the metal, the wood was not as cold.

She turned to Adler. "I know you'll be making a sword. You've apprenticed with a blacksmith and should make something you know how to. As for me, I think I'll be making a bow and arrows. I've always been partial to it."

Adler smiled and walking up to her said, "You've read my mind once again, my love." He kissed her and then went over to the metals, searching for the one that would suit the weapon he was going to make.

Dihni searched the wood, and there in the back of the collection was a set of Ipe wood and next to it a set of bamboo wood. These were the best combined woods for a fast, strong, and light bow. With these two types of wood, Dihni could make a thin bow that could take down the largest of animals.

Dihni rummaged through the sets and chose two pieces that had the straightest lines, of course, it wasn't hard to do with the bamboo. She then took the wood to the worktable and went to search for something to make the string out of. Then she realized that she could make string out of thinned bamboo fibers.

Going back to her table, she found Ilia tying blue ribbon around the ends of her wood.

"Why are you tying that ribbon on the ends of the wood?"

Ilia looked up at her. "The ribbon marks it as yours, no other contestant can tough it. Also, you can't start building till all of the participating contestants are here. Baron is currently putting red ribbon on Adler's materials."

Dihni looked and found that Baron was indeed tying red ribbons on the materials Adler had gathered. "The color of the ribbons matches our shirts. Kegan was also wearing a red shirt."

Ilia nodded. "His issued color is purple, but he refused to wear it this morning, saying he would only wear it at the trials."

Suddenly, curious Dihni wondered what other colors would be used in the trials. "Ilia, what other colors of ribbon should we expect to see?"

Ilia's face scrunched up. "Well, after that group that declined their claims, you should expect to see yellow and orange, I believe. I could be wrong, however, so don't be surprised if you see other colors."

Dihni smiled. "If I see a different one, you'll be the first to know. Ilia, you wouldn't happen to know where I can find an excellent binding solution to put together the pieces of my bow? I would happily use sap, but I think it would take too long to harvest."

An expression of pure amusement lifted the naiad's face, and she took Dihni's hand leading her toward the fireplace closest to the collection of wood.

There, nestled between the wood and the fireplace were four large pots with lids. Ilia lifted one of the lids and Dihni peered into it. The scent of tree sap roes up from the pot, and Dihni smiled at the mass of amber liquid.

"There's so much of it! How is it still so soft?"

Ilia put the lid back in its place. "Enchanted pots. They preserve anything that goes into them in the exact state they were originally in. Tree sap stays soft in this case."

Dihni pointed at the pots. "I need one of these."

Ilia and Dihni both chuckled. Adler and Baron walked up to them just as they started.

Adler beamed. "What's this? Dihni laughing? Ilia you must share this magic you possess." He wrapped his arms around Dihni and kissed her neck. Dihni placed her hands on Adler's arms and settled against him.

For once in her life after Eniha had passed, she felt truly loved by more than one person. It amazed Dihni how drastically different she was now compared to when she felt alone. She wondered if this was what it was like to have family.

Just then, a group of people came into the forge laughing and talking among themselves. As they took in their surroundings, their laughter and talking transformed from simple chatter to exclamations of awe.

Within the group, Dihni saw someone wearing a yellow shirt.

"Hey, Ilia, I see yellow."

Just then, she saw purple behind the crowd and, above it, the smirking face of Kegan.

Dihni's smile left her face, and she immediately was on the defensive. Standing straight, Dihni stood in front of the others.

Adler placed his hand on her shoulder and tried to pull her back, but she would not budge. He persisted, and when it still wouldn't work, Adler stepped in front of her.

"Dihni, he's all the way across the forge nowhere near us. Please ease up a little and focus. You've not only got to make your bow and arrows, but you must use them in front of everyone. If a contestant's weapon fails, they get eliminated. We have to do our best."

When Dihni made no movement, Adler cupped her face and turned it toward his. "For Baron. He's counting on us."

Dihni snapped out of defense mode and thumped her head against Adler's chest, completely baffled by her actions. Adler chuckled and wrapped his arms around her.

"I think you don't like that guy."

Dihni laughed softly and wrapped her arms around him. Looking up into his green eyes, she felt calm and comforted knowing that he was there to help her when she lost control. Adler had been doing it since day 1, and he would continue to do so till they parted ways.

Just then, Baron, who was once again standing on a table, shouted at the large group of people.

"All right! Since we're all here early, we might as well get started! Contestants, some of you have already chosen your materials. The rest of you will be doing so in a moment. Now, when you have chosen your materials, ribbons matching your shirt color will be tied onto them, claiming them as yours. Tampering with ribbons and the materials they are tied onto is grounds for disqualifying. Also, you may only plan out your weapons until it is officially time for the trial to start. If you start working, this is also grounds for disqualifying. Let's get to it!"

Baron jumped off the table and walked back over to them.

"I'm guessing you'll want to plan out your weapons, so we'll leave you alone."

Dihni already had in mind what she wanted to do, and she never planned anything out. If you plan, there's a greater chance to be derailed from the natural course of creativity. Instead, she studied her materials and the way they naturally curved and fit together. She pictured the size of the bow and the way she imagined it would be shaped. Then Dihni thought of the arrows.

Taking a step back, Dihni gasped and looked around. Ilia came up to her, obviously concerned.

"Dihni what's wrong?"

Dihni looked at her. "Please tell me there's a secret stash of feathers I can use for my arrows somewhere in here?"

Ilia laughed. "You are the strangest woman I have ever met. They're in one of the other pots along with some bowstrings made from bamboo. Pretty genius actually, they don't fray and have a terrific snap."

Dihni smiled. "Thank you."

Walking over to the pots, she found the pot that Ilia had showed her before had a blue ribbon around it. Looking at the others, she found another one with a blue ribbon. Lifting the lid, Dihni found two leather bags. Upon opening one, she saw hundreds of feathers.

In the other were the bamboo strings. Dihni put the lid back on and, still smiling and relaxed, turned around, only to be face-to-face with Kegan.

"I see you have help from the locals who also happen to be running this contest. Some might think you have unfair advantages."

Upon seeing his face, Dihni snapped back to full alert and defended herself against his accusing remarks.

"There are no unfair advantages when it comes to friends."

Just then, Adler walked up and stepped between them. The two men stared at each other in a silent war, daring the other to make a move.

"I do believe you have work to do, Kegan." Adler said, his voice implying that he was not being polite but forcing the formality. He took a step forward, and Kegan started to walk away.

"You are correct, Adler. I do indeed have work to do."

Kegan sauntered away to the metals.

Adler turned to Dihni. "I'm glad I needed to come and get a bit of wood. Let's try not to beat his ass and instead beat him in the competition?"

Dihni nodded, not wanting to be disqualified for misconduct.

"You find your wood, and I'll study mine a bit more."

Adler kissed the top of her head and started searching the wood for his special bit. Walking over to her wood and stalk of bamboo, Dihni decided that she would use a leather wrap on the center for a better grip. She made her way toward the leather and found a nice long piece of black leather. On the walk back to her worktable, Dihni looked down and saw something shining in the grass. Picking it up, she found that it was a length of metal in the shape of a long stem with leaves and small flowers. Dihni thought that it would look lovely wrapped around her bow.

Placing her things next to her wood, Dihni found a small bunch of blue ribbons. She tied them onto her materials and the metal.

Just as she finished, Adler come up to her very excited. "Dihni, you'll never believe what I just found it's …" Looking down at her table, Adler paused. He touched the elegantly shaped length of metal and then looked at what was in his hand and back again. Then looking up Dihni, he held out was in his hand to her.

What he gave to her was an inscribrial, a tool that metalworkers used to make a specific design on their weapons like a brand. It was shaped like a brander but was made to leave a mark on metal, not flesh. The strange thing about it, though, was that its shape was of the same flower as Dihni's wrapping metal.

Dihni looked up at Adler and took a deep breath; they had been alive long enough to know that things like this did not happen for no reason.

"We use them. There is no way we came upon these by accident."

Adler nodded and took the inscribrial. His face was the picture of thought. After a moment, he said, "Dihni, what if we are meant to stay here?"

Dihni held up her hand to stop him from speaking further. "One thing at a time, Adler. Keep it in mind, but don't overthink it. Stay focused on the tasks ahead."

She cupped his face and smiled. Then looking behind him, she saw Baron once again on top of a table, crouched and ready to give them the word, staring at his watch.

"You'd better get to your station, Baron's about to give us a countdown."

Adler smiled and rushed off. Just as he reached his things, Baron stood.

"Contestants, begin your work in five, four, three, two, one!"

All at once, you could hear the clanging of metal and the whoosh and crackle of fire as three of the contestants started working with their metals. Dihni looked down the table, on the other side, where the girl in yellow started whittling away at a thick branch. She was probably making a standard bow without any reinforcements or real structure.

Turning to her Ipe wood, Dihni picked up a charcoal pencil and started to draw out the basic shape she wanted the bow to be, making sure the measurements were correct on all sides. Then she took a tool that would gently shave away wood instead of hacking into it.

Luckily, the length of wood she had chosen was almost thin enough and there would not be much done to it.

Dihni kept working the shape of her bow out of the wood. When she finished it, she looked up and saw that it had gotten dark and everyone, except the girl in yellow, was halfway done. She was already bending her bow and making notches for the string to lodge in at the same time.

Dihni shook her head at the simple bow and knew it would not last long. It was too thin and uneven.

Looking back at her work, Dihni tied a blue ribbon on her bow and went to shape the bamboo for her backing. Normally, bamboo would be difficult to work with due to the shape and the way it grew, but this bamboo must have been large because it had no rings and was already split in half and flattened. Someone had been very considerate by going through that trouble for future users. Laying her bow on top of the bamboo, Dihni drew around it for a basic guide on shaping. After setting the bow aside, she chiseled away just outside her markings and was left with backing pieces ready to be glued on and shaped.

Dihni went to the pots and found cups and stiff brushes. She gathered up some sap and a brush and went back to her bow. Using the brush, she spread a good amount on her bow and the bamboo, then gently placing them against each other; she lined them up and squeezed them, then placed clamps to keep it together while she went back and gathered feathers and string. Because her bow was almost Dihni's height, she chose two strings that were the length she would need. Then picking out thirty feathers, which included a few extra Dihni saw something at the bottom of the pot. There, laying under the bags was a container made to hold only one thing. She grabbed it excitedly and opened its rounded top. There inside was a full set of tipped arrows waiting for signature fletching feathers.

Dihni ran over to her work and started prepping the white feathers she had chosen to be put on the arrows. When they were all ready, she took out an arrow one by one and sapped the feathers on, then ties them with a bit of the black leather. There were more arrows than Dihni had feathers, so she tied them with blue ribbon and went back to get more.

As she passed the girl in the yellow shirt, she saw that she was using relatively straight twigs for arrows and had a pile of brown feathers. This girl was not trained in weaponry, and her weapon would fail her.

Dihni felt that she needed to help but knew it best to stick to her own work. After getting more feathers and finishing the arrows, Dihni unclamped her bow and started sanding it smooth using multiple different grains of sanding tools till it looked polished. Dihni then wrapped the center with the leather, making sure it was tight.

Now came time to notch the string on. She made her notching's so that the loops on the ends of the strings would be nestled into the bow and not slip. When that was done, she sanded the ends again and strung her bow.

Testing it and holding it, Dihni was very pleased, but visually, it was lacking. The metal length of flowers Dihni had found was still upon the wood shaving laden table, glinting in the firelight.

Picking it up, Dihni held it this way and that up against her bow, trying to decide how to wrap it on. Finally, she thought of having it on both ends. She put her bow down and tied a ribbon to it, then walked up to the fireplace and took a hot tool out of the fire. Placing the pointed end in the center of the length she waited till it went through and then pounded out the ends flat. They were then dunked into the cold water and taken back to the table where Dihni found Adler waiting.

He smiled at her and brushed the last of her mess onto the ground. "This is amazing, Dihni, I had no idea you were so skilled."

Dihni placed her things on the table and smiled. "Thank you. How is your weapon coming along?"

He beamed and lifted a beautiful double-edged sword. He had used the inscribrial on either side of the blade. The flower vine was beautiful and delicate. The hilt was wrapped in black leather and the end was shaped like one of the flowers.

"Oh, Adler, it's beautiful! You've done very well."

Adler put it in his scabbard, made also of black leather and wood ribbing, and came toward her. He put his right arm around her and looked at her bow and arrows laid out on the table.

"Are you going to wrap those around the ends of the bow? I am allowed to help you."

Dihni thought for a moment. If she let Adler help her, then she would feel as if she hadn't given it everything she had and it would feel unfinished.

"Thank you, but this is something *I* need to finish."

Adler nodded and kissed her. "I'll sit at the end of the table and keep watch."

Dihni turned to her bow and picked it up. Placing one of the vines on the inside, she started bending it around the top once, then twisting it around three times before it ended on the opposite side it had started on. Taking the other piece of the vine, she turned her bow over and did the same to the other side.

To make sure the pieces would stay, she tightened the top and bottom curls a bit more.

Adler still sat and kept watch on the others, so Dihni put her arrows back into the case and strapped it on her waist, holding her bow in her left hand.

Adler stood and looked at Dihni with awe. She looked like an elven warrior getting ready for battle. He looked at the others all of them finished and donning their weapons. Some looked nervous, others cocky, and then there was Dihni, strong and composed.

In Adler's mind, this was no competition, but with Dihni's upbringing, he knew she was avoiding acknowledging that fact. He went to stand by her, and just as he was about to say something, Ilia came up to them.

"You two look magnificent." Then she seemed to take a closer look at their weapons, and an expression of pure wonder overcame her face. She walked toward them slowly and gestured at the vines on Dihni's bow and the flower on Adler's hilt.

"Where did you find those pieces and that symbol?"

Adler and Dihni looked at each other both knowing that this was bound to happen.

"I found the vine on the ground, and Adler found the inscribrial among the tools and metals."

Ilia seemed to look at them with a newfound respect and understanding. She took their hands in hers and looked deep into their eyes. "Whatever happens, do not fail these tests. Those flowers are …" Just then Baron started yelling again.

"All the contestants have finished their work and will now present their weapons. Archers will shoot five arrows into a target, daggers will be thrown into a target, and swordsman will duel! Archers, thrower, to your marks!"

Dihni, Adler, and Ilia walked out into the open area of the forge on the far left was a row of three painted targets made from rounded hay so as not to damage arrows or throwing daggers.

Dihni took her place across the first target, the girl in the yellow shirt stood to her right, and on the end was another girl in green. She had a long red braid that would make any girl envious. Fortunately, Dihni had much-longer hair, but its curly texture made it the same length as her braid, an equal beauty in Dihni's opinion.

Turning her focus back to her target, Dihni jugged how she would have to hold her bow and where she should aim.

"Take aim!"

Dihni pulled an arrow, notched it, and aimed.

"Fire!"

The arrow missed the center by an inch; still in the red wasn't bad. Her goal was the very center black, however.

"Again! Aim!"

Another arrow notched, and her aim adjusted.

"Fire!"

This time, she hit dead center, which was wonderful, but if she wanted to do it again, she would have to split it, and she didn't want to do that. She turned to Baron, who was standing on her left but positioned so he could see all three of us.

"Baron! Might I retrieve my arrows? I'd rather not have to split them to hit the center."

Everyone in the crowd laughed, even Baron, but she didn't even smile. He stopped laughing, and then his smiled turned into an O.

"Yes, of course, go ahead. Retrieve your projectiles, contestants, and run back to the lineup."

She ran, pulled her arrows out, and as she was putting them back in the case, she glanced at the others.

Yellow had her arrows in completely different areas of the target, and green had her daggers side by side in the center.

They ran back to the lineup and took their positions.

"Projectiles will be fetched by Ilia after each center hit. Take aim! Fire!"

Ilia stood on the left and snagged Dihni's arrow, and greens dagger from the center of their targets. Once again, yellow didn't hit center, and Dihni had heard a crack from that last aim.

"Take aim! Fire!"

Just as Dihni's arrow hit center, yellow's bow snapped in half. Yellow looked unsurprised, even smiled, and that's when Dihni knew that she had made an improper bow on purpose. She turned to Dihni, walked up to her, placed her hand on her shoulder and said, "I have never made such a disgrace of a bow, you can count on me being there to help you when you win."

Dihni was shocked; this woman had such belief in her that she had made sure she could give Dihni that message by putting herself out to fail even though she easily could have made it. Why did everyone expect her to win?

A bit shaken, Dihni turned back to her target.

"Esme has been eliminated due to her weapon failing. Dihni, Seif, take aim!"

Dihni took aim and a deep steadying breath.

"Fire!"

She hit center again, and Ilia ran to get her arrow and Seif's dagger. She had two in her hand, which meant Seif had made more than just a few.

"Take aim! Fire!"

They both hit center again. As Ilia ran to retrieve their last projectiles, Baron cleared his throat.

"Dihni and Seif, you will be progressing to the next trial where you will venture to bond and hatch a dragon's egg. Now collect your weapons and shove off, I want to watch a good old-fashioned sword fight."

A great cheer went up, and Dihni went straight to Adler's side. He held her tight and expressed his pride in her then walked to stand in front of Baron. Kegan was already there and looked too eager to beat someone up.

"Now! You two will not be fighting each other but rather these men." He gestured to two men standing behind him to his right. "They are skilled swordsmen and have volunteered to spar with you. Don't kill them, you win when an otherwise deadening blow would have been dealt, or their sword has been thrown from them, and they cannot retrieve it."

He waved them off, and they paired up. Each pair was twenty feet away from the other, and the pairs were standing five paces from their opponents. Adler was to the right, and Kegan was on the left.

"Begin!"

All at once, the ringing of metal and sounds of fighting, as well as cheering from the crowd. Adler's opponent was very talented, as was Kegan's. The only difference was that Kegan's opponent was large and not as quick.

They sparred across the field. And although Dihni tried her best to pay attention, she kept wandering off to a space in her mind where sleep tugged at her. The entirety of the trials, the expectations from everyone, and the implications from the flowers on Dihni's and Adler's weapons had depleted Dihni of her mental and physical energy.

Just then, Baron started yelling again, "Adler and Kegan, that was quite a show! You have both passed the trial and will move on to find yourselves some dragons! All remaining contestants are required to go to their chambers and rest."

Adler's gaze was fixed upon Dihni's weary face as he walked toward her. He immediately held her for a moment and then pulled back enough to put his forehead against hers. She placed a hand on his shoulder, signifying that she was okay but still exhausted.

They turned to leave, and as they started walking, Ilia and Baron caught up with them. Ilia handed Dihni her arrows and smiled. She looked tired as well. Dihni put them back in the case and smiled back at her.

"Wow, you two are amazing. I hope tomorrow goes as well as today," Baron said, still giddy and very awake.

He jabbered on about many things on the walk back to the castle. When they were finally about to part ways in the hall, he paused for a moment, looked them up and down, and smiled softly.

"You two get lots of rest, tomorrow won't be as exhilarating but still an adventure. Adler, you are aware that you can only accompany Dihni this time, right?"

Adler nodded, and Baron slapped him on the back.

"Good man. Now, my love, let's get some much-needed rest, you look absolutely beat." He tenderly wrapped an arm around Ilia and held her hand with his free one.

They walked away with her head resting against him. Adler and Dihni turned and walked to their rooms, his arm still around her. Closing the door behind them, Adler paused to lock it while Dihni stumbled to the bedroom.

Once inside, they started tearing clothes off and shoes, leaving a trail. Then flopped into bed, the covers folded at the end. Adler pulled the covers up and slid his arm over Dihni. Gently holding her as they quickly drifted off to a dreamless deep sleep.

Dragon's Journey

A knock on their door woke Adler from slumber. He lifted his head, whoever was at the door continued knocking.

"One minute," he called.

Looking down at Dihni propped up on his elbows, he quickly assessed that she would not be waking up anytime soon. Adler slid out of the bed and quickly put on his pants and shirt.

Opening the door, he found a blond woman. He recognized her as the woman who had purposefully made that terrible bow.

"What you did last night took guts. Waking us up takes guts too. Can I help you with something?"

She chuckled. "Baron sent me to give you this." She held out a scroll tied with red and blue ribbons. "It's your instructions for the next task. He figured you might sleep in, so he wrote this up for you."

Adler took the scroll from her hand. She smiled, nodded, and then turned to leave. Then turned back around reaching for something in her pocket. "I'd better give you this as well. It's the extra key to your rooms. Baron said it would be best if both of you had one."

Adler closed the door behind him and watched her leave. Then he sat in one of the chairs by the fireplace. Slipping off the ribbons and unrolling the scroll Adler found as set of instructions that were very amusing.

"Good morning, sleepyheads! You missed one fantastic speech this morning, so you'll have to live with this letter of instruction. Today, you'll be setting off to Sena and search for a hatchling. The elder dragon Obiron will be your guide and will meet you both at the edge of our borders. I shouldn't have to remind you, Adler, that you cannot help Dihni in any way, but if you happen to go into the cave of the unhatched and come out with a dragon after Dihni, sweet deal. After you guys get the little flyers,

Obiron will take you to Andros where we'll all be joining hands and singing kumbaya. By the way, on your expedition, if you happen to run into the Raimanos, don't kill any; they'll torment you forever. They are extremely annoying little creatures that love to play tricks on wandering travelers. They look like little elves with large round eyes, pointed ears, and small lips. They are very pretty and graceful.

"Although, you should never be fooled by their features for in my opinion there are little spawns of Loki, a Viking mythical god of tricks. Evil, and terribly cute. Unlike pixies, who are smaller than them and have wings, the Raimanos use birds to fly. The birds love the little buggers, which will never make any sense to anyone.

"Sena is maybe half a day away, and you'll want to go to the base of the mountain. Just follow the trail behind the castle, you literally can't miss it. Have fun! We will be expecting you, I can't say that about the food though, I might eat it all. Oh, and don't forget to collect the eggshells, you'll need then in Andros."

Dihni woke up to find Adler wasn't in bed. She got up and put on a shirt and pants then went out to find Adler sitting in one of the chairs reading a scroll. He was chuckling and didn't notice Dihni coming up behind him.

She slipped her arms around him slowly and kissed his cheek. "What is that? It must be amusing."

Adler held her hands. "It's our instructions from Baron. He is quite young for his age and has a wonderful sense of humor."

Dihni made a noise of agreement as she read the scroll. When she finished, she stood and went to the table where covered bowls of oatmeal and glasses of orange juice and water awaited them.

"We'll eat and then get dressed. It's a long walk, and we slept in. I think we should pack water and food as well."

Adler joined her at the table. "I agree, maybe there will be pie in the kitchen."

They both laughed and continued eating.

When they were finished, they dressed and got food and water from the kitchen. Unfortunately, there was no pie, but there were lots of nuts, dried fruit, and delicious sandwiches. They left the castle through the back entrance from the storage area of delectable edibles. Adler might have taken a few chocolates as they passed by.

They quickly found a trail with an arched dragon carved out of stone above it.

"Baron was right. No one will ever miss this." Adler gawked at it as they passed through. The rest of their walk was not nearly as jaw-dropping. However, on the journey toward Sena, they ran into a group of Raimanos.

The little trickster pulled up thin roots and used them to make trip wires. They mounted their birds and threw nuts and berries at them. Tore at their clothes and pulled their hair.

Today, they just felt like being mean, which Dihni was grateful for, because if they were feeling tricky, Adler and Dihni would never reach Sena in time.

She hoped they had used up the worst of it on Kegan.

Finally, they escaped the creatures after Adler threw most of his chocolates at them. They ran the rest of the way, which wasn't far, and they soon cleared the trees into a meadow.

Obiron, a great golden elder dragon came down from a ledge on the mountain to greet them, stirring a wind that tore Adler's old jacket from his shoulder where he put it after using it to whip at the Raimanos.

With a cry of dismay, he ran after it. Dihni laughed as she watched him.

He looked like a child, tripping and leaping, laughing all the while. His toe caught a rock, and he fell. Turning over, he laughed. His jacket inexplicably landed on top of his face. He snatched it and stood, smiling like an idiot. He held up his jacket and cried with triumph.

Dihni laughed so hard that her stomach started to hurt.

Obiron stood behind her, watching the seen as well. A low rumble of a laugh was rolling through his chest. The sound was comforting.

Dihni turned to him. "Hello, Obiron. I am Dihni Nednepe, and this is Adler Gilfni. I am searching to find my hatchling."

Obiron nodded. "I know why you are here little raven. Climb on my back, and I will take you to the nest of the unhatched."

Adler climbed up Obiron's leg and sat between his shoulder blades and a spike.

Dihni followed him and sat behind him, wrapping her arms around his waist.

"Hold on, everyone, it's going to be a swift ascend!"

Obiron raised his translucent golden wings and jumped beating his wings hard. They rose above the clouds, and Dihni saw a glowing cave in the tallest mountain. They flew fast and reached the cave in a short time.

The landing was not as smooth as their take off. Obiron landed hard and jarred his passengers so hard. Dihni knew they would have neck aches for a few days at least.

Obiron apologized saying that he was not as young as he used to be.

The cave was not lit by fire, but instead was lined with glowing flowers, plants, and moss. Each organism had a different bioluminescence. The effect was colorful and soft.

Dismounting, Dihni stood at the entrance awaiting instructions. Truthfully, she was just stalling because she was nervous.

Unfortunately, Obiron caught on to the scent of her nerves. He chuckled. "You will know when an egg has chosen you for it will start to hatch. Do not fear, little one. Now go, no good will come from waiting."

So she went into the glow.

Inside was a giant room. The high ceiling dripping with flowers and vines from the spikes. Lying around the floor were more than two dozen eggs, each unique. Dihni marveled at the assortment of colors. She walked through them to the center where a pile of cushions and pillows were and sat. As she patiently waited for a dragon to choose her, she hummed a lullaby that Eniha used to sing to her.

Unbidden tears came to her eyes. They brimmed over unwelcome yet bringing relief. She wiped them away and took a deep breath.

A sound came from her right and slightly behind. Dihni turned to see a medium-sized moonstone rocking back and forth only to stop. Confused, Dihni picked it up and set it in her lap. It fit perfectly just inside her knees.

Then it occurred to her that it may have responded to the lullaby and had stopped when she had.

Not wanting the egg to explode on her, she set it down and began humming again. The moon stone started rolling and cracking once more, it bumped into a green egg close to it and then rolled away from it. Part of the shell popped off, and she saw a little snout.

The scales were silver, and yet they were opal with hints of blue, it quivered as the creature sniffed the air. The snout disappeared, and Dihni saw a blue eyes staring out at her. Then it too disappeared, and the egg burst apart, revealing the shimmering little dragon. It crawled out of the mess of shell bits and goo, shaking from head to tail and stretching out its wings. Then it looked up at Dihni and slowly came toward her.

Picking up her melody, Dihni sang, and the little beast crawled up and clung to the front of her shirt. Dihni smiled, which made him wiggle and start crawling all over her.

Dihni started laughing and shrieking, which made Adler trot in. He paused to marvel at the cave and then made his way over to crouch in front of Dihni.

He smiled. "I see you've found yourself a little friend."

As Adler was reaching out to let him smell his hand, the variscite egg he had rolled into started to shake.

Adler reached out for it. "What the …?"

It suddenly burst apart, and an emerald dragon with silver highlights lay on its back with wings spread open. It chittered and struggled to roll over.

Adler laughed and reached out, helping the little one on its feet. "There you go. Well, what do you know? You're a pretty little thing, aren't you?"

It chittered and stumbled over to him. Picking it up, he held the little creature tucked against him and petted its head. Adler beamingly looked up to see Dihni absolutely flabbergasted.

"You're never going to believe this, but he bumped into the egg of that dragon you now hold before he hatched."

Adler chuckled. Little Green looked up and saw Dihni, then looked past her, and saw little opal peaking over her shoulder. They both got very excited at the sight of each other and leaped toward the other. Spinning and tumbling around the floor, the two chittered and made baby roars.

Dihni and Adler laughed watching the two plays.

"Best friends before and after hatching. My love, it was meant to be." He reached out and took her hand. They stood up together.

Then Obiron peeked his head in. "If you four are quite done playing about, I'd like to see the littlest ones."

Adler and Dihni picked them up, and just as they were about to walk away, Dihni thought of something.

"Adler, the shells."

He stopped. "Oh, right! Let's collect the pieces quickly."

They pulled out their leather pouches and collected every bit of shell then left the cave.

Obiron smiled. "Well, now, you two are lovely. You'll make fine dragons."

Little opal snorted, and Little Green chittered happily.

Then Obiron looked at Dihni and Adler. "There is something you must know. I sense a connection between these two, and when they get older, that connection may turn into something more."

Adler and Dihni nodded, knowing exactly what he meant.

"Do you know what you will name them?"

Adler petted Little Green's head and smiled. "Emerald. My little Lasy Emerald."

Obiron turned to Dihni. She looked down at the little beast in her arms and could not think of a name.

Looking back at Obiron, Dihni shook her head. "I do not know what to name him."

Obiron nodded. "It will come to you. Now, let's be off to Andros to meet with the others. We should make it in time for dinner."

And so another task was completed, and they must move on.

Climbing onto Obiron's back proved to be more difficult with the dragons, but they made it up into their spots.

Dihni moved her dragon onto her shoulder where he clung to with all four feet the entire flight. The flight was smooth, and Dihni decided to shape a bit of shell into an egg. It was about the size of her thumb and would make a lovely necklace.

She wrapped it in a bit of cloth and stored it in the pouch with the rest of the shell pieces.

Just as the sun started to set, they reached Andros.

Fairy Dust

The fairies greeted them with hellos and welcomes. A group of Kelie were there as well cheering when they saw that both had hatchlings. Baron ran up to them and stared openmouthed and ecstatic.

"I see you went in after Dihni! They are amazing. What did you name them?" He reached out to try to pet Emerald. She did not approve and snapped at him. Adler admonished her and told her to be nice.

Looking up at Baron, he said, "This is Lasy Emerald. Dihni has yet to name her hatchling." He looked at Dihni and smiled. "I'm sure it will be a unique and meaningful name, one that requires forethought."

Dihni deeply appreciated his understanding statement. Lasy Emerald was a perfect name for her, but Dihni wasn't sure of her dragon's rightful title yet.

Baron placed his hand on Dihni's shoulder and turned to the crowd. "Dihni has a hatchling and is entitled to continue on. Adler has also been successful and has a dragon of his own. Kegan and Dihni will be tested by the fairies' light tomorrow. One of them will be granted wings, the other will not, thus determining who will be crowned prince or princess, later to become king or queen!"

The entire crowd cheered, and it took a moment for them to settle down.

"Now, each of the contestants that have been eliminated will be on the royal court, including tomorrow's elimination. The courtiers will be allowed to choose their areas of expertise and can either live abroad or in our homeland. Now, let's get back to whatever we were going to do after this!"

Everyone laughed, clapped, and went back to their business. Baron turned back to them. "Now if you guys will excuse me, I'm going to go find my lovely wife and some more food. Farlan here will be your escort and guide." He gestured to a fairy with pale tan wings to his left.

Farlan smiled at them. "Hello. As Baron said, I'll be accompanying you. I imagine you'll be wanting food and refreshments, as well as to mingle?"

Adler and Dihni looked at each other. "Food, drinks, bed?" Adler asked.

Dihni nodded. "I think so." She turned to look back at Farlan. "Lead the way, good sir."

Farlan led them to a table filled with fruits, vegetables, nuts, salads, and a few meats. There was also wine and juices, along with water, of course. After filling their plates and cups, they settled down next to a large tree to eat. Sharing food and enjoying every morsel. The dragons especially loved the meat and berries.

"So, Farlan, what is your role in fairy society?" Adler asked.

Farlan finished chewing and swallowed before he answered. "I am a weaver. I make our spider silk hammocks, as well as anything that would go with them. Pillows, blankets, rain covers, you name it."

Dihni scooched forward half an inch. "Did you say spider silk hammocks?"

Farlan chuckled. "Yes. When woven properly, it's very strong, waterproof, and temperature friendly. No overheating. No getting too cold."

Adler took a few nuts from his plate. "Will we be sleeping in these hammocks of yours?"

Nodding, Farlan pointed up in the tree. "It's funny you would choose to sit here. This tree is where you, Baron, and Ilia will be sleeping. They requested you all stuck together."

Looking up in the branches of the mammoth tree, Adler and Dihni saw four hammocks. Two of them were set lower, and the other two were higher up. The hammocks glinted in the light; the silk sparkling.

"Oh, Farlan, they're beautiful."

"Why, thank you, Dihni. They are indeed eye-catching in the fire and moonlight."

"Admiring Farlan's handiwork I see," Ilia said.

She was walking up to them hand in hand with Baron, a small smile on her face. They settled down on the ground next to them. Ilia reached over and took Farlan's hand.

"Thank you for keeping them company while we attended things."

Farlan nodded and smiled.

Adler put his hand up. "Hold on, I thought you said he was our guide?"

All three of them laughed. Baron answered while still chuckling. "He is, but tonight he was just company. We knew you'd want to go to bed, but we didn't want you wandering around alone. So we asked Farlan here to guide and keep company. He's a good friend."

Everyone laughed some more. Then Dihni's dragon curled up in her lap and fell asleep.

"The little one is right. Time for bed. Farlan, it was lovely to meet you, I look forward to sleeping in your wonderful creations. Adler, will you join me this time in climbing the tree? It may not have apples, but it has hammocks."

She laughed cradling her little creature and jumped into the tree. She landed on a branch and climbed the last few up to one of the higher hammocks. Adler made his way up and settled in beside her.

They couldn't reach far enough to touch, but it was all right. Sleeping apart was not going to change anything. Obiron slept on the ground among a mass of flowers. Dihni ran her hand along the tight weave; it was like they were sleeping in silk.

Dihni's little dragon slept curled up on her chest. His scales shone brightly in the pale moonlight. She looked over to see Emerald lying on top of Adler's head, her tail laying across his eyes. A thought came to Dihni: she had not named the little beast yet. The way he had hatched, his shining scales—these things she thought of, and a name came to her.

She whispered, "I shall name you Lunairus."

Lunairus did not stir and slept soundly. Sleep soon found Dihni, and she drifted off.

The next morning, Dihni awoke to Baron swinging her hammock. "Wake up, sleeping beauty! Whoo! No biting."

Lunairus did not appreciate the rude awakening and nipped at Baron's fingers. He let go and wagged his finger at him. Putting his hands back on the branch he was sitting on, he chuckled at Lunairus.

"If you had a name, I'd scold you with it."

"Lunairus, no biting … hard."

Baron laughed. "Well! Lunairus, your charge is awake. Oi! Adler! Where's my money?"

Adler laughed. "You still have one minute to get her out. She may have named him, but the other half of the bet was that you could get her out of bed in three minutes!"

Dihni scrunched her eyes at Baron. He held his hands up smiling. She rolled her eyes and with them rolled out of the hammock. Baron yelled in alarm; Adler looked up the tree and saw Dihni falling down the tree swinging from branch to branch. She landed solidly next to him. Lunairus clutching onto her back.

"Good morning, lovely."

Dihni stood there with her hands on her hips silently scolding him for the bet.

"Oh, stop, it was all in good fun. Don't try and tell me you wouldn't have done the same to me."

Dihni smiled and gave him a kiss. Meanwhile, Baron plopped down beside them.

"Dihni! Stop jumping from high places and scaring the life out of me!"

Dihni looked over Adler's shoulder and laughed. Adler turned and started laughing too. Baron stood there with twigs, leaves, and other debris stuck all over him and in his hair. Coupled with the exasperated look on his face, he was an amusing sight.

He picked at and wiped away everything with their help, and then they went off to eat breakfast. This time, the tables were filled with bread puddings, fruits, vegetables, nuts, juices, water, and salads. No meats, pies, cheese, or simple toast.

At some point, Ilia joined them. Dihni hadn't even noticed her slide in next to Baron, she was too in raptures with the delicious bread pudding. Then a fairy with purple wings flew down out of the giant tree they were all seated in front of. She held up her hands, and everyone quieted down to listen.

"The queen sends her greeting and laments her not being here. She wishes the contestants best of luck. It is now time for the contestants to step up and present themselves. Dihni and Kegan, please make your way to the fairy circles at the base of the tree."

Dihni and Kegan followed her to the base of the tree. There they looked around, the entire girth of it were many rings of mushrooms. Dihni stood in front of one; Kegan on another.

The fairy landed in front of them and gestured with her hands to each of them. "You both have hatchlings, and if you followed your instructions, you should both have the eggshells with you. You will place every bit of shell in the circles. If the shell burst into dust and reforms itself into something else, you will be allowed to step into the circle yourself. This will prove that you and your dragon will be able to receive fairy magic, you are both connected, and therefore you will both have it. Empty your shells into the circles."

Dihni took out the bag of shells and then the carved bit she had wanted to keep and placed them in the circle. Kegan did the same with his. When they stood up again, the fairy held her hands over the circles, and the mushrooms began to glow. The shell pieces lifted off the ground and slowly spun around, then they burst into speed and collided in the center of their vortex, bursting apart and turning to dust. Kegan shouted in fury for his pieces had merely lifted and then fallen back to the ground.

Then the dust gathered itself and started to form. It shaped into a beautiful medallion and chain, long enough to fit over her head without a clasp. The medallion had the small egg shape in the center, and surrounding it was an intricate dragon, its wings tucked in.

The medallion flouted toward her, and Dihni reached out and took it. It still had the beautiful colors and shimmer the shell had.

"Put it on, give your dragon to your partner, and step into the circle."

Dihni turned and handed Lunairus to Adler, he watched from Adler's arms where he and Emerald nuzzled into each other. She stepped away putting the medallion on and looking into Adler's eyes, afraid of what this meant for her but accepting it nonetheless.

At first, nothing happened, then the mushrooms brightened and her feet rose off the ground. An orb of light bobbed in front of her. Its color was changing, flitting through all the colors, and finally settled on a pale blue with darker hues strung through it.

It then rushed straight at her and in to the center of her chest. She felt a surge of energy and cried out for it felt like someone had torn open her back and was pulling and shifting her muscles. Featherlight bones and strong muscle protruded from her back and her skin stretched across them. Then wings started to grow. She could feel new nerves spreading to the tips of them and it tingled as if they were asleep.

As the light faded, she lowered to the ground slowly. Her dragon wriggled himself free from Adler and ran, half flew over to her. Adler followed him and fell to his knees next to her.

"Dihni, my love, are you all right?" He touched her cheek, and her hand felt cold compared to her feverish temperature.

"I am fine."

Her gaze was not on Adler but on the bright-blue gossamer wings unfolding behind her. She gave them a few experimental beats and gasped at the new sensation. Dihni fluttered them, and she rose off the ground to a standing position.

Adler stood with her, making sure she didn't fall. They smiled at each other. Gaining confidence, Dihni slowly rose into the air and then shot up and swooped over everyone in wide circles, laughing. She landed next to Adler smiling like a child who just got a much-longed-for present.

"What is your gift, child?" the fairy asked.

She was everything strong and compassionate. She had defied the odds all her life even when it was her own life at stake. She had fought for the well-being of others. There was no true, intentional selfishness within her. She was a warrior. She was a leader, She was a teacher. She was a friend. This was her gift. To be everything she already was with a bit of magic to help her along.

"My gift is many things, but most of all, my gift lies with the people."

Baron and Ilia walked up to them, not as a friend would, but as respectful and humble officials.

Baron broke his serious gaze for two seconds to give them a stupid smile and then cleared his throat.

"Dihni Nednepe, you have passed every trial with a humility and calm I have never seen before. Adler Gilfni, you have stood by Dihni and helped her every step of the way, never getting upset about being on the outside. You both have shown great leadership skills and have proven your right to rule over these lands. The bonds that were forged with each of them have shown that you are willing to coincide with their inhabitants as well."

He looked at them both and then at the weapons they carried.

"There is one other thing. Adler, Dihni, the materials you found in the forge that had flowering vines on them. They are the symbol of Izzalatia, the crest of the royals. It is no mere coincidence that you were the ones to find them. When the people of Izzalatia abandoned their home, the crest vanished, along with anything bearing its symbol. A legend told that when the time came, the king and queen would find the crest and reclaim the throne. You did find the crest, and now you have reclaimed the throne!"

The crowd burst into cheer; the fairies and even Obiron joined in as well.

"We must celebrate! Let us feast and plan an official coronation!"

Dihni and Adler stood still as everyone went back to the tables to feast. They looked at each other, and Adler smiled.

"You're not surprised at all, are you?"

Dihni looked back at the people—laughing, eating, and having a wonderful time.

"Not one bit. By the way, these made me starving." She fluttered her wings a bit, and Adler laughed shaking his head.

"It's going to take a while to get used to you having wings. They are stunning though. Another part of you that adds to your already mesmerizing beauty."

Dihni's insides turned into a puddle, and she leaned against him. He bent down, cupping her face, and kissed her sweetly.

A few cheers, whistles, and catcalls resonated from the crowd. They broke their kiss and went to join the party. They feasted well into the day, and then decided that it would be best to go back to the castle. Some groups had already left, going through another portal pool. Ilia and Baron were about to head through with a group of their own.

"Will you come through the portal, or would you like to break in your wings?" Ilia asked with a knowing look upon her face.

"You know very well that I want to fly. We'll see you at the castle." Dihni gave Ilia a hug. Then they looked to where the boys were talking enthusiastically and then bear-hugged each other.

Ilia chuckled, and Dihni looked at her quizzically.

"Ilia, you wouldn't happen to know why they are being so exuberant, would you?"

Ilia smiled, still looking at them. "Actually, I do. See Baron just told Adler a very exciting bit of news."

Dihni was staring at them, trying to get an idea of what they were talking about, but she had no clue.

"He just told him that we're expecting a pondling." Ilia looked sideways at Dihni.

Dihni couldn't contain herself. "I KNEW IT!" She jumped and squeezed her arms around Ilia. She could hear the boys laughing and shouting.

Ilia gripped Dihni. "Dihni, now, I know you're excited, but could you please put me back on the ground and stop spinning before I get sick?"

Dihni hadn't realized that she had flitted them both two feet into the air and was indeed spinning. She immediately stopped and gently set them back on the ground.

Baron held on to Ilia, and Adler wrapped his arms around them all.

"I really want to get back, but this is such a perfect moment."

"Baron."

"Seriously?"

"Oh, honey!"

Adler let go of them, and they all laughed walking toward the portal pool where Obiron was watching.

"Congratulations. I'm positive you will be wonderful parents."

"Thank you, Obiron." Baron patted his leg, and then the two jumped into the pool and swam under.

Adler climbed onto his back, Emerald on his shoulder and reached down for Dihni.

"Oh no, you don't. You have wings of your own now, little one. You'll be flying on your own." Obiron jumped into the sky, refusing to let Dihni protest.

Dihni let Lunairus situate himself between her shoulders before she flew after them. Now that she was actually in the air, Dihni was glad Obiron refused giving her a ride. The wind rushed through her hair and pulled it back into a flowing wave behind her. Her wings were nothing but a hummingbird's blur of glittering blue.

Looking at the ground below her, she marveled at the speed of which it passed by beneath her. At this speed, they would reach the Izzalatia by sundown. Looking over, Dihni found Adler was smiling like a buffoon and staring at her.

She flew over them until she was hovering over his head. If she reached down, Dihni would be able to touch his dark mop of hair. Adler never lost focus on her and tried to grab her. Dihni easily dodged his hand laughing.

"If you two would stop playing about, you would notice that we're here."

Dihni looked down to see the brightly colored trees that grew atop the castle. They were shaping the flower crest as if one giant flower were blooming beneath them.

Obiron landed in the forge to give himself enough room not to damage anything. Adler dismounted, and Dihni landed next to him.

"If you ever need anything just call on me, and I will answer."

Then he took off and flew back to Denet. Adler and Dihni made their way through the people in front of the castle toward the tables where Dihni loaded a plate and then ate while they made the journey to their room.

When they reached the door, Adler unlocked it and let Dihni in. She finished what was left on her plate and set it on the table then walked into the bathroom.

"I'll start drawing the bath."

Adler was headed toward the bedroom. "You go ahead, I'll catch up with you in a minute."

Dihni turned on the water undressed, and got in. The tub quickly filled up, and Dihni was very relaxed from the hot water. She sat up and dipped her wings in. It felt strange having nerves protruding from her back, but it also felt wonderful, and she sank into the tub up to her chin.

Adler came in to join her. "I would say someone is very tired."

Dihni sighed in agreement. They lay in the tub for at least twenty minutes before Adler finally got out. He then reached down and pulled Dihni out he had a towel around his waist and one cleverly draped over his shoulder so that Dihni could lazily pull it over herself.

He carried her like that into bed where he took her towel and dabbed at her wet wings. Then he covered Dihni with the blankets and crawled in.

In the time that it took to get her and her wings dry, she had fallen asleep, and now he just lay there gazing at her. There was no doubt how much he loved her, and he fell asleep peacefully with his heart overflowing.

Celebrations and Coronations

The next morning, they were being fitted into their coronation outfits. Dihni wore an elegant, open-backed, long-sleeved dress that was currently pooling at her feet. The dark-purple silk made for an interestingly beautiful puddle. As the seamstress pinned it up and hemmed it, Dihni sighed; looking in the mirror, she admired the pop of blue her wings gave the dress.

Adler was in another room being fitted into his suit, which was also the same dark purple. He was given a blue cloth for his breast pocket and a blue tie to match Dihni's wings.

Dihni held out her arms as another seamstress worked on her sleeves. It was getting tiring lifting and putting down her arms so much, but she was grateful they were taking such care to get it right.

"Is it almost finished? I can't wait to twirl and look like a giant cupcake."

The seamstresses laughed, then the woman who was at her feet said, "Almost done. I'm on the last few inches, and Reanna is finishing off the last sleeve."

Dihni looked in the mirror at her long flowing curls and tilted her head.

"Do you think I should do something with my hair? Maybe pull a few tendrils back and make a small braid?"

Reanna finished off her sleeve and looked at Dihni's reflection thoughtfully, then at her hair.

"I think that would be lovely, I'll do that right now."

She started pulling curls back and braiding them, leaving a few smaller curls to frame Dihni's face. Then she pulled a purple strip of silk from the scraps and tied it around the end of the braid.

She smiled into the mirror. "Beautiful."

The other seamstress stood. "Indeed. I believe you're ready and with time to spare. How about that twirl now?"

Dihni grinned and stepped away, then started twirling. Her dress billowed around her and flowed. Much to her delight, she looked like a giant cupcake.

Just then, Adler walked in and started laughing. Dihni stopped twirling and was giggling herself.

"I've never worn such a beautiful dress, I couldn't help it. What do you think?"

Adler smiled at her with such love that she thought he might melt. He looked dashing in his suit, his green eyes and black hair making him the most handsome man she had ever laid her eyes on.

He held out his hand. "You are an absolute vision."

Dihni took his hand, and he pulled her up to him, twirling a small curl around his finger and then trailing it down her face.

"You look mighty dashing yourself. Purple suits you."

Just as Adler was about to kiss her, Baron came in and whistled at the sight of them.

"Well, don't you two look cool? I'm wearing white, and you guys are decked out in purple."

Dihni and Adler turned to see that Baron was indeed wearing a white suit with a green pocket scarf and tie. Dihni was a bit shocked to see him so spiffed up.

"Why, Baron, you look fetching. Is Ilia wearing white and green as well?"

Baron fussed over his jacket and tie and nodded. Once he stopped fidgeting, he looked up at them and took a deep breath.

"Well, everyone is gathered up, so you might as well come down."

Baron promptly turned and left. Dihni and Adler looked at each other. They both took a deep breath and walked out the door, down the stairs, and down the hallway to their left toward the throne room.

Dihni looped her arm through Adler's and leaned her head against it as they walked. Adler stopped and turned to Dihni making her stand up straight. He even bent down to look her dead in the eyes.

"We can do this. There have been much-greater things that we have done in the past. I know that we have no experience running a kingdom, but I've led armies, and you have the academy. We'll make it one day at a time, and we won't be alone."

Diani wrapped her arms around Adler and held tight.

"Thank you. I've been bothered by this ever since the forge. I am no longer bothered, nervous yes, but not afraid."

Standing tall and turning toward the doors, they gathered themselves and waited for the doors to open. Inside the room, they could faintly hear Baron making a speech. Then the doors opened wide, and the sound of bells greeted them.

The entirety of the Keli was filling the room from corner to corner, dressed in silken clothes in every color but purple. A long aisle led straight to a set of thrones beautifully carved with brightly colored cushions, where Lunairus and Lasy Emerald perched on the backs.

All around the room were dark-blue banners that bore the flower symbol of the kingdom. The ceiling and walls were covered in vines, some of which bloomed the very same flower and others blooming the glowing flowers that they had seen in the cave of Denet.

There were accents of gold everywhere, on the banners, the cushions, and even some of the Keli were wearing gold or gold accents. The entire back wall of the room behind the throne chairs was made of windows, letting in lots of sunlight.

Dihni and Adler started walking down the aisle, and as they passed, the Keli bowed and curtsied. Baron and Ilia stood at the bottom of the steps where the thrones sat. Behind them was a pedestal, and on the pedestal rested two crowns. They were delicate and silver, shaped in long twists with a gentle point down the center. One was ever so slightly thicker and bigger, but they were identical.

When they reached Baron and Ilia, the bells stopped chiming. Baron looked up at the large group of people then back at Dihni and Adler.

"Diani and Adler, you have proven your right to claim the thrones of Izzalatia and stand before your people ready to lead them. I believe you worthy of the task, but if there is anyone who says otherwise, this is the time to say so."

"I say otherwise!"

A gasp and murmurs went out through the crowd, and there, stepping out and into the aisle was Kegan.

"Kegan, on what grounds do you say they are unworthy to rule?" Baron wore a scowl upon his face.

"On the grounds that they are unwed and such a rule is without a solid foundation."

Baron looked at them in shock. "Is this true?"

Adler stood straight as a rod. "It is. However, marriage is nothing compared to the bonds of Ohet Ma."

The crowd refused to be silent until those words came out of Adler's mouth.

Baron looked at them, one then the other, back and forth, and smiled. Then he looked up at Kegan who looked as shocked and dumbfounded as everyone else.

"Then, Kegan, I do believe you have no grounds to say otherwise on their crowning."

Kegan stumbled back into the crowd.

Baron looked back at Dihni and Adler. "Dihni, Adler, do you swear to protect your people, uphold Izzalatia's traditions, and maintain the peace to the best of your abilities?"

Dihni and Adler answered in unison. "We do."

Baron smiled and turned to pick up Adler's crown.

"Adler Gilfni, I crown you our brave, wise, and fair king."

He placed the crown on Adler's brow and stepped aside. Ilia then took his place and stood before them and turned to pick up Dihni's crown.

"Dihni Nednepe, I crown you our true, strong, and loving queen."

She placed the crown on Dihni's brow and then stood next to her husband.

Dihni and Adler walked up the steps to their thrones and sat down. The entire assembly burst into cheer and applause. Lunairus and Lasy Emerald screeched above them, attempting their first roars.

The king and queen held hands and smiled at each other. Then Dihni turned to the assembly.

"Please dance, eat, drink, and celebrate."

A band set to the right of the thrones struck up a lively song, and people dispersed around the room. Some of them danced, others went to the tables around the room, and still some lined up to speak with the new queen and king.

Most of them gave their congratulations, some pledged fealty, others asked questions about their plans for the kingdom. After three songs, there was no one lined up, and Baron once again took his place at the bottom of the thrones.

"Ladies and gentlemen, it is now time for the king and queen's first dance."

Adler stood and held out his hand to Dihni. She took it, and they walked to the center of the room where Adler bowed, and Dihni curtsied. Then the band started playing a lovely tune of strings, bells, and flute. It was a traditional Izzalation tune.

Adler and Dihni stepped, spun, and leaped in the traditional dance they had been taught. It was quite fun, and they beamed with joy. The song ended with Adler holding Dihni's waist with her hand on his cheek, her right arm resting at her side.

The gathering of Keli clapped, and Baron stood on the first step.

"Ladies and gentlemen our king and queen!"

The celebration lasted all the rest of the day, and by nightfall, people had slowly trickled out till they were all gone. Ilia, Baron, Adler, and Diani decided to go to the kitchen where they asked the cook to make them potpie and blackberry pie.

They sat and enjoyed their meal, laughing and soaking in one another's company when Ilia reached across the table and took Dihni's hand. She looked her dead in the eyes, squeezed her hand,

and said, "This is everything your mother wanted for you. To have friends, a soul mate. To love and be loved."

A single tear slid down Dihni's cheek, and she smiled at Ilia.

"I'd like to talk about her more every chance we get."

Ilia nodded. "Of course."

After they had their fill of pie and were ready to go to bed, Baron and Ilia pulled out two keys out of nowhere and handed them to Adler and Dihni.

The keys had the Izzalatian flower on them.

"These are the keys to your new chambers, which are just slightly bigger with two other study rooms, a bigger bedroom."

Adler looked at Dihni and smiled at her like a giddy kid. Then he stood up and bolted for the door. The others laughed and chased after him. He, however, had used all his speed and was already at the doors when they caught up to him, impatiently waiting for them.

"Hurry up!"

Baron laughed out loud, and Ilia giggled, whereas Dihni shook her head and smiled.

"Dude, I know your excited, but remember, we've got a little one to keep in mind. Speaking of which, we helped decorate your rooms, so we will let you two alone and go to bed."

Adler and Baron hugged while Dihni and Ilia embraced. They said their good nights, and then Adler pushed open the door. He had previously unlocked it and opened it slightly before they had gotten to him.

Adler and Dihni were not expecting the sight that lay before them. The door opened into a room decorated with the furniture from Dihni's castle that had been refurbished.

Dihni stepped back and gazed at everything, then ran to a door on the right. It was a study filled with things she didn't recognize. She ran out and through the door, opposite it on the other side of the room, she found a study filled with her books, table, chairs, and rug from her room at the academy.

Going back into the sitting room, she found a door to her left. Upon opening it, she found her bed—a larger hutch than in the other room they had, and another one right next to it.

"Adler, everything from the academy is here, isn't it wonderful?"

Adler was standing in front of the fireplace looking above it, tears streaming down his face. Above the fireplace was the painting of her parents, and next to it was a painting of two other people she didn't recognize.

"Adler, honey, are those your parents?"

Adler sniffed and nodded.

"I don't know how they did this, but I am eternally grateful. It's been so long since I've seen their faces."

Dihni wrapped her arms around his waist and looked up at the painting. The woman had Adler's eyes and his black hair. The man looked like an older version of Adler with gray hair and brown eyes.

"You look like them. I'm sure they would be proud of you."

Adler looked away from the painting and down at Dihni.

"Your mother would be proud of you as well."

They looked at the paintings and hugged for a few minutes, then decided it was time to go to bed. After hanging their clothes so as not to ruin them, they set their crowns in the locked boxes inside the hutches. The boxes had small silver keys on top that they used to lock them with.

After this, they crawled into bed and couldn't help but get a little tangled. Afterward, they cuddled in an exhausted and warm embrace.

"Dihni," Adler asked after a moment.

"Yes, Adler?"

"Will you marry me?"

Dihni opened her eyes and was over him in a hot second, staring him down.

Adler was smiling like an idiot. A beaming smile broke her face.

"Yes! Oh, my Lanta, yes!"

Adler sat up and wrapped his arms around Dihni. Then he flopped back down as he kissed her passionately.

The Wedding

A week later, Dihni was being fitted into her wedding gown made from beautiful sheer white fabric with a touch of baby blue in it. The back was open with a strap above her wings. The skirt was short and lightweight, and it flowed in the breeze from the open window. An overskirt was open to the front and trailed behind her in gauzy wraps. The sleeves were long and were pointed on the back of her hands, looped onto her middle fingers.

Her hair had small braids and twists in it and had been put up in a flowing royal ponytail. A colorful butterfly pin sparkled in Dihni's hair, along with blossoms from a harmony vine, which was what they found out the Izzalation flower was called. The makeup upon her face was light and brightened her natural features.

Looking in the mirror, she raised her wings and saw that she would never look as beautiful as she did that day. Committing the sight to memory, Dihni took the bouquet of flowers from one of the flower girls and stepped off the pedestal just as a knock came at the door.

"Come in!" she called.

A servant walked in with Lunairus trailing behind him. He was holding a big slice of meat, and Lunairus was practically drooling. Lunairus was wearing a black bow tie and had a basket in his mouth. Inside the basket was a small red pillow; on the pillow lay two rings.

Dihni beamed from ear to ear. "Lunairus, look at you. You are so handsome. Come here and let me take a closure look at you."

Lunairus ran over to her. The rings were tied to the pillow, and he didn't drop the basket. When he reached her, he turned in a slow circle and lifted his head high. It was not the first time he had listened to a simple request and done all her other requests without her asking. Dihni marveled at their connection and was excited to see what they would accomplish in the future.

"Thank you for getting him ready, Rupert."

Olivia, Dihni's lead maid, came in the room beaming. "My lady, it is time."

Dihni smiled. Olivia rarely called her "my lady" but by harmony. She had not figured out why Olivia called her that.

Taking a deep breath, Dihni walked out across the hallway, down the stairs, and out the door toward the gardens. Flower petals blew through the open doors and were strewn across the floor. Images of what their life would be like after this came into her mind.

As she stood there, the bridesmaids and groomsmen walked out in pairs. Ilia and Baron going first as they were maid of honor and best man. Then after the couples, it was Lunairus, and he strutted out. Diani could hear the *oohs* and *awes* and smiled, the dragons were such a hit. Then Dihni's cue came, and she stepped into view, lifting her wings to catch the light.

As soon as Adler saw her step into the light, he thought he might die. He placed a hand on his heart as it burst with love.

Adler looked dashing in his blue-gray suit and white shirt. His hair was still as unruly as ever. Reaching out, he took Dihni's hand.

"Dearest guests and loved ones, today we witness the marriage of our bonded king and queen. You may ask why a bonded couple would want to have a marriage title, well as special as a bond is, so is marriage. The bride and groom have prepared a few special words for each other."

Adler took both of Dihni's hands and looked at them, rubbing his thumbs on the backs of them.

"The first time I held your hand, I never wanted to let go. The first time you spoke to me, my heart broke. I couldn't imagine life without your voice. Seeing where you've come from, knowing what you've been through, and how you've changed so much from that place of solitude and sorrow, I am so grateful to have witnessed it. Dihni, you are my one true love, and I want to forever keep witnessing the changes life brings you, the changes that life brings us."

Adler teared up a bit, and Diani did too.

"I love you so much, Adler. When you called me down from that ledge and took me into your arms, I finally felt at home and safe. I was confused and defensive at first because I had never before experienced that feeling, but then I understood what it meant, and I opened up to you. The more we spent time together, the more I fell in love with you, and then I took you to my tower, which in a way was my heart, and we shared our first kiss there. The moment you called me down and held me was the moment you set me free. It was the moment our love was created."

Adler had tears; Diani had tears; guests were crying and sniffling, including the minister who tried his eyes, cleared his throat and kept going.

"Adler, do you pledge to be faithful through every trial the two of you may face. Through sickness and in health, so long as you both shall live?"

Adler smiled and squeezed Dihni's hands. "With all my heart, I do."

He slipped Dihni's ring onto her finger.

"Dihni, do you pledge to be faithful through every trial the two of you may face. Through sickness and in health, so long as you both shall live?"

"With every bit of me, I do."

Dihni slid Adler's ring onto his finger.

"I now pronounce you man and wife."

Dihni and Adler shared their first kiss as man and wife as the assembly burst into laughter, cheering, and clapping.

They spent the rest of their lives together, running the kingdom. Eventually, they had children of their own.

Aedan was their firstborn, a strong young man with dark hair, pale skin, and yellow eyes that border on orange, and gold in certain lights. They named him Aedan because of those fiery eyes. He has fire in him; therefore he was born of fire. He looks very much like his father and is just as tall.

Their second-born is Fawn; a beautiful little girl with long dark hair, pale skin, and giant violet eyes. Her large eyes reminded them of a deer and her small delicate frame of a fairy. Fawn is still very small but is not to be underestimated.

Aedan chose a room that had a passageway door beside his bed. He was always sneaking around in the passageways.

Fawn chose a room that had more bookshelves in it than walls. Connecting it was another room that held her bed. Fawn spent most of her time outside running on the roof of the castle.

Adler and Dihni rule Izzalatia and her subjects with all the love, respect, and discipline she needs. Fawn and Aedan will soon lead the academy and travel through the portal pools often.

Ilia and Baron had a little boy named Cornelius, who is Aedan and Fawn's best friend. All the parents secretly hope Cornelius and Fawn will end up together.

THE END

About the Author

By Jordyn Owen
https://www.jordynowenphotography.com/

I'm a 20 year old who happens to be a massive daydreamer and hopeless romantic. I've loved writing stories and reading my whole life.

CPSIA information can be obtained
at www.ICGtesting.com
Printed in the USA
FFHW021235300319
51319840-56801FF

9 781643 509877